D0686299

TIME

Unwanted

Isaac Betancourt

Copyright © 2021 Isaac Betancourt

All rights reserved

This book or any portion thereof may not be reproduced, used or transmitted in any manner whatsoever to include without the express written permission of the copyright owner except for the use of brief quotations in a book review.

This is a work of fiction. Special events are mentioned to suit the story. With the exception of public figures, any resemblance to towns, persons living or dead is purely coincidental. The awful acts done in the book by the characters, it is strictly their doing and not the author's.

ISBN-13: 9798755179645
ISBN-10: 1477123456

Cover design by: Author
Library of Congress Control Number: 2018675309
Printed in the United States of America

For Rubia

"Every new beginning comes from some other beginning's end."

— *Marcus Annaeus Seneca*

table of contents

I THE PLAN

The Mockingbird laughed at her. She was sure. Helen heard that mockingbirds mimicked noises like car alarms, but laughing? Ridiculous! How can such a sweet bird laugh so diabolically if not mandated by the devil? Did the bird know what she intended to do?

Helen wondered how long she dozed off. Her eyebrows sprung upwards toward the ceiling in hopes the movement would help her wake up. She yawned and turned to the television. The appliance showed children laughing around a dining room table with a colorful cereal box in its center. It annoyed her.

She reached for the remote that she found on the wooden floor. The large, white rubber buttons made it stand out. Helen wondered how much time had passed. Helen suddenly realized she had fallen asleep during the "test" process. Part of the "test" meant to find out how loud the television could be late at night without her neighbor or the police knocking on her door. The volume was intolerable, even for her. Helen liked to control her surroundings. She often called her space "controlled chaos."

"Damn me!" Helen exclaimed aloud. She had been planning this for some time to mess it up now. She calculated she slept for about 45 minutes. Perhaps, she wondered, "is this a passive-aggressive way of sabotaging my plan?" The self-destructive behavior started to take over and grew like a nasty fungus. Maybe guilt was to blame, she guessed.

Her mood improved when she realized no one knocked on the front door, no cops. That was great news. She could execute her plan without worries. Practically, she could make as much noise as she wanted, without anyone suspecting a thing. Her mother would die tonight.

A bunch of cops showing up at the house would be a concern. The more, the worse. She knew how troublesome that would be logistically. The crime would most likely go thoroughly unchecked at night. Helen found police resources were severely scarce after dinner time. Her research consisted of going to the source itself, the police.

Helen had falsely reported a stolen bicycle at the station. She flirted with the desk officer on duty that evening and easily obtained the answers she wanted. The officer was curious about her motives but dismissed her questions as another local fascinated with cops. To her delighted surprise, he revealed only three patrolmen worked after hours. The low number would work well in her favor.

＊ ＊ ＊

Helen rushed to the kitchen and glanced at the old cuckoo clock. She lamented as she always did that the cuckoo stopped functioning. The clock had been there for as long as Helen could remember. She shook her head in disapproval, telling herself she should've repaired it long ago--only for sentimental reasons--good thing it still gave the time.

Perhaps the cuckoo had grown tired. "We all become tired sooner or later, buddy," she mumbled. "Unlike me, at least you did something. You were smart in quitting early."

Helen had been overwhelmed by life. Until recently, she had never seen a therapist. The stigma in town is that only the dysfunctional would be the ones to seek psychological help. Only so, when forced to do so by impatient family members or the courts. Otherwise, the belief was, you should toughen up and move on.

She regretted going to the appointment. Right before the one-hour session ended, the therapist expressed surprise as to why Helen had never sought psychological help before. That made her feel inadequate. At that precise moment, Helen decided never to return. She would not be vulnerable.

Helen's difficult childhood seemed too much for the therapist to bear. The therapist apologized for Helen's misfortunes more than Helen wanted to hear.

The therapist tried to sugarcoat the diagnosis by telling her she would most likely suffered from Complex Post-traumatic stress disorder.

Helen told the therapist how her mother turned into an abusive alcoholic. She had self-medicated with alcohol after Helen's dad died in a motorcycle accident. Helen was seven years old at the time. Shortly after that, her mother started having strange weekly reunions with peculiar people.

"About ten to twelve of them, every Saturday evening, for months would bring jars to the house filled with a red substance that looked like blood. They would also have bird feathers, incense, and mushrooms. I would hide behind the curtains and watch.

They would lay one person on a table, eat the mushrooms, use the feathers to cover the person's chest with the blood, and loudly chant in unison in Latin, "vita in morte sumus!" Which meant, "in death, we live."

"Interesting," the therapist said, wanting to say instead, "that's odd."

"Mom would frequently call my dead father's name, "Colton, Colton, when her turn to use the feather came, and plead to him to speak to her. Then the man on the table would pretend to be my dad. Mind you, the man's voice was way more bass-like than my dad's. The man would tell my mother how much he missed her and that they would be together again soon. My mother would then sob every time. I didn't feel bad for her. I thought she liked torturing herself with the illusion.

She forbade me from watching, telling me I was too young to understand. There was this one time she caught me hiding behind the curtain, grabbed me by the hair so forcefully; it ripped a chunk right out. I started bleeding with blood running down my forehead.

My mom then yelled at me to go back to my bedroom. The others immediately dissuaded her, telling her that the virgin's blood would be excellent for the ritual. She nodded. They placed me next to the man already lying on the table. With their feathers, they took the blood from my forehead and rubbed it on his chest."

"How awful," said the therapist." One day, they stopped coming," said Helen without missing a beat. "I guess my mother eventually grew tired of the charade. I never asked why."

❄ ❄ ❄

Helen's idea of committing murder sparked more than a year ago. Back then, the plan came like a whisper, devilishly humble. She imagined herself getting rid of her as the days went by. The excitement started accompanying her thoughts. Within weeks, an unremorseful tornado wanting to wreak havoc inside of her grew, convincing her to free herself at any cost. What first seemed to be a crazy thought transformed into a very viable plan.

"I'm not a murderer," she had said many times, trying to convince herself against it. She failed.

Her attempts of reassurance she was not the murderous type did just the opposite. It sprung both imaginary scenarios and dry runs -- that always ended in worst-case scenarios -- which often flipped into best-case situations, where she would go free.

Nowadays, every minute of every hour, Helen desired to release herself from the life of servitude that she despised. Her youth eroded in that house. Elizabeth had gaslighted into being her caretaker. Helen hated herself for her inability to have boundaries and her extreme codependency.

Helen wanted more than anything else, even more than she wanted to be with her lover Paul, to be a woman free of burden.

Sure, her efforts had not gone unnoticed. It brought unwanted recognition that now she could use to her advantage after the murder, especially from Carmen, her nosy neighbor.

Carmen was a Puerto Rican woman who spoke English with a heavy Spanish accent. She stubbornly moved permanently with her soldier son after Tropical Storm Nancy ravaged her home in Puerto Rico. Carmen spent her time alone. The military deployed her son to retrieve reusable military equipment left in Vietnam.

Carmen was lonely. She told Helen every chance she got. Helen thought because of Carmen's desperation for social interaction; Carmen would strategically position herself to be outside of her house when Helen would be. Helen could not understand the need to be around people. For her, the less, the better.

Carmen would find a way to listen to Helen while on the phone. She would stand there touching the hibiscus plant that always appeared thirsty and with drooping leaves.

Helen would tolerate Carmen because, honestly, she was suitable for her spirit. Carmen would always start their conversations with, "I don't know how you do it, Mija--taking care of your mother for so long. I'm sure Dios," and while pointing her index finger up, "has a place reserved for you right up there, in heaven."

Helen liked the recognition. It was validating to know others were agreeing she was making a considerable sacrifice.

Carmen referred to herself as an "old school" Puerto Rican. She was a devoted Catholic woman who understood the English language but never felt comfortable speaking it as she seldom used it back home on the island. She described her English as a self-made mix of English and Spanish. She had named it "Carmenspanglish." She explained her Spanglish was more sophisticated than ordinary because it had words only, she knew.

She would use a made-up term if she didn't know how to say something in English. Like the time she had asked Helen to help her with the "Raccoondilla" in the backyard. She told Helen the creature looked like "an experiment gone very wrong. A possible human-made mutant and horrendous looking animal."

"Racoondilla?" What is that?" asked Helen.

Carmen responded with a condescending look on her face as if Helen should've known, "you know, a mix of a raccoon and an ardilla."

"A mix of a raccoon and a squirrel? I have to see this!" Exclaimed Helen knowing with her high school Spanish what "ardilla" meant.

Skeptically, Helen grabbed her father's old rusty shotgun she kept behind the fridge for "just in case."

She followed Carmen, and once they got to the rear of the house, Helen couldn't hold her laughter when she found a frightened possum, desperately looking for an opening in the fence to flee out of their sight.

"Ay Mija, we don't have those on the island," said Carmen while raising her hand dismissively and going back into the house.

* * *

Helen's stomach growled. She hadn't had anything to eat for the past day. She dismissed it as an unnecessary annoyance. A means to an end. "An end, how fitting." She thought. Helen placed her hand on her abdomen, assuring herself it was the right thing to do; for her, the baby, and her future with Paul.

The thought of Doctor Paul Thomas felt like an oasis in the middle of her life's chaos.

"Rarely romance goes without drama," Helen told herself, meaning some bad things must occur first for good things to follow suit. She wondered where Paul was and missed him. The idea of being together instilled the reassurance she needed to move ahead with the plan.

"I'm not a killer," she told herself again before walking to her mother's bedroom.

She opened the door quietly. The dated hallway lamps shun a yellow light inside, revealing the body covered by a stained white sheet. One would've never noticed the curtains nailed to the wall to prevent any opportunity of sunlight intruding in if not by the nail's rusty heads.

Her mother, Elizabeth, slept. The room smelled of fermented urine.

A small lamp on the night table provided weak illumination. It made the room look older, like a daguerreotype photo. Helen turned on the light at random times and would shout out a good morning! To confuse Elizabeth if it were day or night, she had started doing it a few months back, and to her surprise, it did not take long to fool her mother.

It had also helped that Elizabeth had voluntarily sequestered herself in the room. A few times, Elizabeth told herself, "with everything that's going on out there nowadays, there is nothing to see and nothing to miss. I've lived it all anyway."

Paul agreed to untruly diagnose Helen's mother with a weak heart at Helen's request. They both knew Elizabeth would be afraid to die anywhere but home.

Helen tiptoed towards the digital clock on the night table that showed the time to be 8:36 PM. She cautiously pressed the set time button, changing the clock to display 8:36 AM.

Helen had been waking her mother up in the middle of the night to give her oatmeal. Elizabeth always woke without protest. Helen felt relieved she didn't have to argue about that. It would make things a lot easier when the time came.

The truth was that Helen could've saved herself a lot of hassle and just dispose of her while she was asleep. But for this, more than the act itself, she needed to feel she fooled her mother, that she was the one in charge and had total control.

Helen started looking forward to the kill.

* * *

Helen had been an only child. Her father, Colton, worked at a motorcycle repair shop. He had rented the shop from a friend who had quickly become tired of the business. Most of the bikes were American. Colton would fix those to include the occasional British bike some youngsters would bring in.

Most bikers looked down on any motorcycle brand other than Harley Davidson. Colton himself didn't care much about brand exclusivity other than fixing Harleys helped his business stay afloat. "A bike is a bike," he would tell his clients. A usual grunt of disapproval by some would follow.

The town teens would bring their Triumph motorcycles left in barns by their grandpas after World War II to try to get the thing started. Colton would fix them for free if not too complicated of a job. Sometimes, it was as simple as cleaning the old carburetor of the old gunk, and the bike would start right up. Colton enjoyed seeing the youngsters' faces lit up with excitement.

Elizabeth was a staying-at-home mom. She smoked "like a chimney" when Colton wasn't there because he hated the smell with a passion. She kept whiskey bottles hidden under the living room floorboards and occasionally brought a bottle out to take a few sips. "Southern whiskey only for me," she would often say. In the beginning, when Helen happened to see her doing it, Elizabeth threatened her with a "good belt beating" if she dared say anything to anyone. A few months later, Elizabeth drank unconcerned as Helen watched.

Elizabeth could barely stand when the police showed up at the door. The officers had a hard time understanding her slurred speech. Elizabeth fainted once she found out about Colton's death. The alcohol odor about her was so strong an officer unintentionally uttered, "Jesus, lady," while trying to get her to regain consciousness. The officers weren't sure if Elizabeth had blacked out from the alcohol or the shock of the news.

Colton's Softail had not been a match for the truck that hit him head-on on the Foaming River bridge. The driver told police he was looking down at a map at the time of the crash. He swerved into the opposite lane, and when he saw the one headlight, it was too late.

Colton was buried with military honors as he had served in an aviation unit in Vietnam. Elizabeth stood over the casket after the crowd left, watching as they lowered it into the hole. The grave diggers begged her to go, but she refused.

Once they filled the grave, she walked away.

Elizabeth never found out what Colton was doing at the bridge at that time of day. He was done with work and nowhere close to home. She always attributed it to an affair but never was able to prove it.

Afterward, Elizabeth submerged herself into alcohol until the money ran out a few months later. She closed the business and sold his tools at a fraction of what he paid. With no income and the looming threat of losing the house, she joined a church group that agreed to pay her bills as long as she entered a rehabilitation program. She joined, stuck with it, and never drank again.

II THE CURSE

Helen often dreamed about sharing a space with Paul permanently. She liked to imagine herself residing in a Neoclassical-style house with the cars parked on a circular driveway. The daydreams provided her with the escapism she needed from negative thoughts and insecurities--obstacles to complete the plan.

"Honestly, it's not like I want to kill her," Helen thought. "I deserve a better life. I want to have a relationship without being concerned about people finding out about Paul and me. I will be wealthy and without a care in the world."

Elizabeth was asleep. Helen gently turned the knob to exit the room quietly.

The faint sound of the song playing in the kitchen's small, dated radio made Helen smile. The song was one of her favorites. She sang along. When the song ended, Armstrong Bluemoon came on the radio," ladies and gentlemen, the track you just heard was Dawn go Away by the Four Seasons."

Helen liked '60s music. It reminded her of better times. She often fantasized about flirting with service members who wore bomber leather jackets, rode loud motorcycles, and found her undeniably irresistible. The thought made Helen feel pretty. She always ended the fantasy with a short giggle. The same way she felt when thinking of Paul.

She trotted to the kitchen like a young girl playing hopscotch, although a few gray hairs placed her two years shy of her 20th-year high school reunion.

Helen stopped and stood in the kitchen in front of the sink. She searched her left pocket for the piece of paper that became a comrade in arms, never leaving her sight. She found the note buried under a small Sony tape recorder.

A yellow pencil, engraved with a faded black number 2, also emerged from the pocket to rest on the kitchen table. The paper's consistency was weak due to constant use. Helen was a superstitious woman. Helen thought that rewriting the list on another piece of paper would mean she would be starting the plan all over. She desperately wanted this chapter in her life to end.

Helen unfolded the paper on the table. She went

down the list. Her index finger moved like when hovering over an Ouija board. She took the pencil out of her teeth and placed a checkmark next to number two. The number one had a faded check-mark.

My freedom to do list,

1. Cut her nails (Scratching is never good)

2. Set the clock (Night=day)

3. Obtain the pink bowl from the kitchen (oat-meal)

4. Prepare the oatmeal

5. Grab your favorite spoon :)

6. Pillow (The one in the red flannel case)

7. Vomit? (Disgusting, I know)

8. Kill :(or :)?

9. It must look natural

10. Call 911

Helen told herself that having the list was a dangerous thing to do, yet significant. She thought that being organized was imperative for success to get away with a crime. "As idiotic as it may sound," she often told herself, "it is best to follow every step to stay focused."

Just like anyone committing a crime, she guessed, carelessness could lead to sloppiness. In turn, sloppiness could signify a successful conviction in a court of law. She had seen it over and over while watching crime shows and documentaries. The ones that got sloppy always got caught.

Helen opened the white pantry's door and took the instant oatmeal box that read "Brown Sugar." She emptied a packet into the pink bowl, adding water and cooking it for a minute on the stove. "Not too cold, not too hot," she instructed herself, mocking her mother's voice while attempting to sound neurotic.

Helen grabbed the bowl and searched for a spoon. Per her list, she would use her favorite one for this occasion, inscribed with the initials "HB" for Helen Baron. Her mother gave it to her on her sixteenth birthday. Helen looked for the spoon in familiar places, the kitchen drawer, the dishwasher, and the glass cabinet. "Where in the hell?" she asked, becoming frustrated. After rummaging through the kitchen drawer again, she found it concealed under other spoons. The silver plating had faded, mainly revealing a copper surface.

Helen grabbed the paper and pencil, placing checkmarks next to the numbers three through five,

3. Obtain the pink bowl from the kitchen (oatmeal)

4. Prepare the oatmeal

5. Grab your favorite spoon :)

She placed the list and pencil back in the pocket of her green sundress.

The oatmeal resembled quicksand. Helen touched the bowl, and the temperature seemed right.

"Might be on the colder side, but it'll do," she said. She walked back to the bedroom and turned the knob while simultaneously kicking the door open. The door slammed against the wall, making a racket.

Her mother raised her head off the pillow with an annoyed look on her face. She gave Helen an angry stare. "What the hell is wrong with you, Helen? Don't you see I'm asleep, for God's sake!!" said Elizabeth loudly.

"Never mind that sleepyhead. Time to wake up," said Helen in a psychopathic playful tone while pointing to the red numbers on the clock. "Look at that! Oh my, is it morning already? I need to give you breakfast."

"Morning already?" Elizabeth said. She looked at the clock that read 8:43 AM.

Helen smiled wickedly. She sat next to the bed and mixed the oatmeal in the bowl. She then grabbed a spoonful.

"Just the way I like it?" Elizabeth asked in a suspicious tone. "Did you make this?" Elizabeth looked at the spoon, immediately closing her mouth tightly in disapproval.

Elizabeth's neuroticism wouldn't be abnormal for someone that knew her well. If they did, they would know Elizabeth liked history. Roman history, to be exact. In comparison with ancient times, she thought the modern world was not significantly different. She told Helen she feared having the same fate as a Roman empress, poisoned by someone in her inner circle or worse, by a family member.

She was of the firm opinion that receiving food

cooked by someone else meant there was always the possibility of becoming a victim, a dead one. For that reason, she disliked restaurants very much, "you never know what happens in that kitchen unless you cook the food yourself," she would often say. "That is why you often read about how important food testers are." With a shrug, she would finish telling Helen, "Rich people have them, you know."

Helen heard the same argument countless times. She would tell her mom to get off her high horse, that she was not of such high status, for someone to want to hurt her.

Helen mixed the oatmeal one more time, "rest assured, Mom, there is absolutely nothing to worry about. No poison here," she said.

Helen reflected on what she was about to do. "It's not the food you have to be concerned with," Helen said under her breath. The spoon made a clunking sound in the bowl, "and yes, to answer your question," Helen said aloud," I made the oatmeal just the way you like it," replied Helen, "not too cold, not too hot."

"Are you sure?" asked Elizabeth.

"Yes, mother," replied Helen condescendingly.

"Okay then, get on with it," commanded Elizabeth.

Helen showed a fake smile. The same one she used frequently. It had not been hard to pretend when the person on the other side brought nothing but hardship. "Patience," Helen thought, "it will all be over soon."

Helen took a spoonful and put it in her mouth. She moved it around several times, filling her cheeks before swallowing it. Elizabeth frowned while watching in disbelief. Helen grabbed another spoonful and put it in her mouth once more.

"What's gotten into you, Helen?" asked Elizabeth. "Why are you eating my oatmeal and using one spoon for both of us? You know how I'm not too fond of it. It is disgusting!"

Helen did not answer. She wanted to stay on track. Helen took care of her while others moved on to build successful careers, marriages, and happy lives. Her mother had been abusive and selfish. Helen's wasted away in a bedroom full of old Mahogany and unpleasant smells. The days full of tedious repetition had become an all too boring scene.

Helen stopped herself from feeling guilty. After all, the doctor wrongly diagnosed her mother. You could say that Paul was to blame. She would've gone about her life if he had not violated his Hippocratic Oath by starting a relationship with his patient's daughter.

The motivation for the fake diagnosis had been multifold. Helen could stay home, he could stop by anytime he wanted to "check" on her mother, and their affair would go unnoticed. It had been status quo until three things happened; she fell in love, wanted much more than their occasional encounters, and got pregnant. She hadn't told him the last part.

Helen looked at the wooden Jesus-less cross her mother kept above the headboard. "God will eventually forgive me," she thought while swallowing more oatmeal. She believed she earned her place in heaven. But regardless, at this minute, there was no room for more reflection. It was time for execution.

Helen stopped eating the oatmeal and held it inside her mouth without swallowing. She dug the spoon in the bowl and stuffed it in her mother's mouth.

Helen's breathing intensified, preparing to do it finally.

Her anxiety had been building and was now becoming unbearable. If she didn't act soon, she would start hyperventilating like she did when things worried her much.

Her hyperventilation seemed to become worse lately. Paul tried dismissing it but had finally given her a prescription for anti-anxiety medication.

Helen's cheeks were full of oatmeal and, like a balloon, deflated when she swallowed. Elizabeth couldn't resist now but to question Helen about her behavior. She was still hungry, and her daughter had eaten her meal.

"Helen, what's wrong with you? You are acting so strange!"

Helen stared at Elizabeth without answering. Elizabeth persisted, "can you please tell me what is going on with you today? You don't seem like yourself." She watched Helen place the bowl on the night table.

Helen grabbed the last spoonful and started to drive it into her mother's mouth. Elizabeth became repulsed. Her hunger prevailed, and she swallowed. She wondered about Helen's behavior and what was behind her absent stare.

Helen got the paper and pencil out of her pocket and silently read the next item on her list, placing a checkmark next to it,

6. Pillow (the one in the red flannel case).

Helen's breathing became calmer. She was getting closer to her goal of becoming a free woman.

"Today, of all days, you notice I don't appear like myself?" Helen started while grabbing the pillow from the floor. She was working herself up for the kill.

"Let's start by recalling how you decided to lay on this bed after dad died. You chose to stay in this room while having me take care of you all of these years."

"But the doctor was the one who diagnosed me," replied Elizabeth.

Helen interrupted, "let's not forget how you drank my childhood away. You allowed those cult men to take advantage of me. You had no issue keeping me here all of these years."

"Helen..." started Elizabeth.

Helen interrupted, now turning toward her with the pillow in her hands. "You know what? Being your only daughter was my punishment. I could not live a decent life, love, or spend any happy time outside these walls because of you."

"You have the nerve of blaming me?" Elizabeth said in a tone of disbelief. "How dare you?"

"You held me here under a lie," Helen said. "You have no Congenital Central, whatever the hell the name is. Paul told me the truth. You are a healthy woman. It is all in your head. I have to free myself, and for me to be able to do that, you have to go."

"Go? What sort of mind games are you playing?" asked Elizabeth. "That doctor diagnosed me. You were here! How could he have told you that I'm lying? That is preposterous!"

Elizabeth paused and frowned, "wait a minute, what do the two of you have planned? There's something you are not telling me."

Helen pointed at the cross on the wall, "the time has come for you to pay for your selfishness, mother."

"Helen, can you please explain to me what's going on?" asked Elizabeth, becoming frightened. Helen did not respond.

"Helen?" she called.

Helen exited the room. Elizabeth heard the television come to life with a news anchor reporting about John Lennon leaving the Beatles. Helen came into the room. Elizabeth then asked, "John Lennon left the band?"

Helen couldn't believe her ears. She shook her head and grabbed the pillow—the one in the red flannel case.

"For heaven's sake, Helen, what's going on?" begged Elizabeth.

Elizabeth was about to yell for help when Helen put the pillow against her face. She struggled. The instant lack of air gave her a burning sensation in her chest that drove her to instant desperation. She panicked. Elizabeth's brain sensed the need for air and sent signals ordering her to do anything possible to survive. She tried frantically to uncover her head and breathe, but the pillow pressed firmly against her face.

Elizabeth reached for her daughter, flapping her arms in mid-air with her right hand, grabbing Elizabeth's left bicep. The fingers dug into the skin but caused no damage. Helen cut her mother's nails very short in anticipation.

"Why? But why?" thought Elizabeth. Helen pressed harder.

Elizabeth accepted she was losing. The seconds moved like a giant's enormous foot coming her way to crush her. She started to be swept by a less than hopeful darkness, overwhelming any chance for life and future.

Many times, Elizabeth thought her life was not worth living after her husband's death. She felt empty, yet she had never pondered dying. And now, it was all clear; she was about to die. Helen, her only daughter, was killing her.

Elizabeth started to drift in and out of consciousness. The neurons that managed both sides of her brain were now fighting but losing their stronghold. They began to flicker like defective light bulbs.

Some people have said that at this moment, right before death, they see their life flash before their eyes. Instead, Elizabeth wondered how Helen planned to get away with killing her. She must have thought of a way out.

Elizabeth had an instant realization; her suspicions about her daughter having an affair with the doctor were true. Yes, the evidence was now irrefutable; the giggles, the whispers, the late-night sounds coming from Helen's bedroom.

She now knew she was an obstacle Helen had to vanish. Elizabeth wondered if the doctor knew. He had to. Was her diagnosis a lie? She had trusted him. Hence the reason she had turned a blind eye to all the shenanigans.

Elizabeth calculated she had maybe, at the most, a few seconds left. Time was running out, "time, time!" She thought. "I need more time!" She wanted to think some more and figure it all out.

Elizabeth became enraged. The love she had for Helen turned in that instant into a dark and un-forgiving sentiment that had no room for alternatives. She decided that she would use her last straw of energy to curse her daughter. The spirits would listen.

Elizabeth screamed words under the pillow that Helen was not able to understand. "I CURSE YOU, HELEN!" Elizabeth uttered. "I CURSE YOU THAT JUST LIKE ME, YOU DIE BY YOUR OFFSPRING!"

Elizabeth's brain systematically shut down like a fuse box blowing up its circuits one by one. The heart was the first to go. Then the lungs. The brain was last to die, waiting stubbornly a few minutes before giving up all hope.

Helen noticed Elizabeth stopped struggling. She held the pillow for a moment longer to make sure her mother was dead. Once satisfied, Helen threw the pillow aside. It landed on the floor, sliding forward and stopping at the wheelchair.

Helen was panting from the struggle. Her forehead was sweaty, and the front of her hair was now wet falling on top of her eyes. She gathered it and made a low ponytail.

Helen told herself she had to remain focused. She let out a huge sigh and shook her hands in front of her to gather her thoughts. She placed the spoon in the back of her throat, forcing herself to vomit while opening Elizabeth's mouth wide.

The vomit erupted quickly, exiting swiftly and in a larger quantity than she expected. The vomit filled her mother's mouth and ran down her right cheek like unstopping viscous lava. Helen tried to stop the liquid from reaching the bed, but she wasn't quick enough.

"Oh well, not part of the plan, but I'll be able to explain," Helen mumbled. She thought of cleaning the mess but decided it would look more natural not to.

"Has to look like my mother choked," Helen thought. She inserted the spoon in her mother's mouth, shoving some of her vomit down the throat. She put the spoon in her mouth and licked both sides to clean the oatmeal before placing it back in the bowl.

She looked at her mother's body. Elizabeth's eyes opened as if staring at the red pillow on the floor.

III THE GOOD OLD DOCTOR

Helen walked to the kitchen. She washed the bowl and the spoon, placing both upside down on the counter so the two would dry. Helen grabbed the phone on the wall and took a deep breath to allow herself to channel a grieving daughter before dialing 9-11. She perceived she was getting anxious. She would be careful. The call would undoubtedly show her tone and demeanor if the investigation ever came to that point.

Helen dialed 9-11. The phone rang two times. Before the third, someone clearing their throat came on the line.

"Edom Police Department, what is your emergency?" said a male voice.

"My mother," said Helen in a distressed tone, "something is wrong with her. She is not breathing."

"Okay, ma'am. Has CPR been performed?"

"Yes," lied Helen.

"What's your address?"

"962 Sweetgum Way."

"Can I have your name?"

"Helen, Helen Baron."

"How do you spell the last name?"

"B, as in bravo, A, as in Adam, R, as in rich, O, as in oleander, N as in nothing," Helen thought she sounded too casual.

The man typed furiously.

"Hi, Helen. My name is Robert, and I'm here to help you. I'm sorry you are going through this. Can you tell me a little more about what happened?"

Helen thought Robert sounded like a nice man. She smiled and wished she knew him. "Well, I was feeding my sick mother, as I always do at night, when suddenly she started vomiting. Then it looked like she was choking. The next thing I see, she passes out, and she stops moving," she said, adding, "oh, and then I did the CPR thing."

"Are you okay?"

"I'm upset but fine."

"Is there anyone else in the house?"

"No. Only me and my dead mother."

Robert thought that was an impersonal way to refer to her mother.

"How old is she?"

"She is 63 years old."

"Is she suffering from any conditions?"

"She had heart problems."

"Okay, thank you."

Robert typed some more, "so she is not moving?

"Nope," Helen said, sounding almost happy.

"How long has she been suffering from this?

"For several years now. Doctor Thomas has been treating her," Helen stated.

"So, your mother is not breathing, you say?"

Helen faked a sob. "I'm pretty sure she's not."

"I'm so sorry," he told her in a compassionate tone.

"Thank you," Helen said. She wished the call was over. She so desperately wanted to call Paul.

"Can you feel a pulse?" inquired Robert.

"I'm not in the same room she is now. I can't check without putting the phone down. The phone cord is not long enough. But if your question is if she's alive, I can tell you she looks pretty dead," Helen sounded impatient.

Robert stopped typing. "Please try to calm down, Helen," he said. Helen thought the advice was unnecessary; she was perfectly calm. "The ambulance is on the way. I assure you the medics will do everything possible. "Stay with me," Robert paused. Then immediately corrected, "stay on the line."

"Okay," replied Helen.

Helen heard the faint sound of sirens in the distance. "They are coming," said Helen, "I can hear them now."

"Okay, very good," said the dispatcher. Helen's breathing intensified as the siren noise grew louder. She wondered if they would find out what she had done.

The sirens stopped blaring. There was a vigorous knocking on the front door.

"I have to go," said Helen hurriedly, "they are here."

"Very well," said Robert, "goodbye, Helen."

"Goodbye."

Robert hung up. The red light on the call panel turned green as it stopped recording the call. Her story had been saved, among the remains of thousands of other calls forgotten by time, waiting only to serve as evidence of a crime.

"Coming!" Helen yelled.

She reached for the familiar paper and pencil and wrote a number 11, followed by the word "done." Instead of carefully folding the piece of paper as she had done for months, she crumpled it and stuffed it in her pocket as she ran to open the front door.

* * *

In the late 1800s, a civil war veteran named Robert Nichols searched for a piece of land that would resemble his image of the perfect place to call home. He told himself that he would know it when he saw it. It was the middle of fall. He came upon a piece of land to the north populated by sweetgum trees with leaves that had turned bright red. He described the place as finding "a sunset in the middle of the day." For that, he named it Edom. He settled there, and instantly another American small-town was born.

The town of Edom in North Carolina was small and quiet. The 70s had been good to it. The job rate was high, and the townspeople were content with life there. The pace was slow, and people went about their business without worrying too much about anything. Most that were born there stayed there. With a few thousand people, everyone pretty much knew each other.

Doctor Paul Thomas was one of those characters everyone knew. His family had lived in Edom for generations. They were famous and highly respected for being the ones responsible for saving the town when the paper mills left. They started by organizing steeplechase races that eventually started attracting wealthy horse owners.

Eventually, the event evolved into thoroughbred races bringing bigger wallets and bigger prizes. The Edom Stakes had become known as the southern second-most popular horse racing event after the Kentucky Derby. The town joke was that there were more horses there now than people.

For Paul's grandfather, saving the town in the early '50s when many considered it on life support had not been easy. It had taken a lot of dealing and wheeling. Most farmers had run out of means to continue their craft without consumers buying their produce. The closing of the paper mill also meant there was no market for their timberland trees.

Their land sat unfarmed. Paul's grandfather

visited the skeptic farmers. He told them he would personally put money in their pockets equal to what they would make in a year's farming if they agreed to lease their land to board horses. The farmers had no other option but to agree.

Paul's family had gambled their prosperity. They had won their gamble with the nationally recognized Edom Stakes.

The doctor was a town celebrity. He was charismatic, had the money and influence, and could do no wrong in the eyes of the townspeople. Paul was the only doctor in Edom that practiced general medicine at his small office on Main Street. Most of his childhood friends thought there was no money in general medicine and pursued surgical careers instead.

For Paul, a surgery career had not been an option. Money was no issue, and he liked the attention he received from helping others. His wife often joked sarcastically that his primary love language was acts of service, but not for love.

Paul had tried the big city life. Upon a schoolmate's recommendation, he opened a practice in Malibu after finishing medical school at Stanford. That's where he met Catherine. She was attending the Malibu school of Arts and was doing street sketches to support herself. She was pretty good. Paul had noticed her beauty and talent. He had agreed to get his drawing done as an excuse to ask her out. He did, and eventually, they married in Edom. After the wedding was over, she wished never to return to Edom. She missed their life in Malibu.

They had been married for almost five years. Three years ago, they had relocated to Edom when Paul's father had discovered he had advanced Prostate cancer. A month after Paul and Catherine settled in his parents' home, he passed. Paul's mother begged him to stay and start a new medical practice in Edom. He agreed. Catherine protested to no avail.

For Paul, the decision had not been hard. On the contrary, it had been an enormous relief. Although the money was good in Malibu, there was no comparison to having the full support of his family and the admiration he craved from the townspeople.

Catherine hated riding with him in the car. As he would drive around town in his convertible, single women threw kisses; some married ones winked, and the men saluted as if he were a war hero. He enjoyed his fame.

She found him to be presumptuous and arrogant. Catherine argued that offering free medical care to some should be done for altruistic reasons, not to fuel the ego.

"You have no idea what you are talking about," would respond Paul in a dismissive tone. "That's not how the real world works."

Catherine was growing increasingly tired of the small-town life. Paul's long hours, coming back in the middle of the night while she pretended not to notice, and his sikken attitude toward their relationship was making things worse. She had started to think of moving back to what now had become their beach house in Malibu.

* * *

Catherine found the constant ring of the phone annoying. She refused to get up.

"If I get up and this is a wrong number, I swear I will kill someone," she thought, removing her blanket.

She turned and looked over at Paul. He was sleeping, his back facing her. The flip clock on the night table showed 10:47 PM.

The ringing paused for a few seconds, and then it resumed a few seconds later.

Paul turned and lifted his body upright. Half-awake, he asked, "who could be calling at this hour?"

"I don't know Paul, you tell me," said Catherine in a suspicious tone.

Paul ignored her tone. "Cat, can you please get it?" He shortened her name every time he wanted something. "I have to be at work early. There is this pregnant patient, and she can only come at 7:00 AM."

The phone kept ringing. "Catherine? Please?" said Paul, now looking at her while frowning.

Catherine went begrudgingly downstairs to the kitchen and lifted the receiver. "Hello?"

"Can I please speak to Paul? I mean, Doctor Thomas?" Is he there?" asked the woman on the phone. Catherine recognized the voice. The same woman had called the house, asking Paul for advice every time she felt her mother wasn't doing well.

"I recognize your voice," said Catherine in a tone that asked, "what in God's name is so important that would make you think it is okay for you to call us at this forsaken hour?"

"Is there an emergency?" asked Catherine.

"I must speak to your husband immediately," said Helen, sounding desperate.

"What's your name again?" asked Catherine.

"Helen."

"Hold on," said Catherine while placing the receiver on the table.

Catherine grabbed a glass of water and walked upstairs.

"Paul?" called Catherine.

Paul turned toward her, "yeah? Who is it?"

Catherine gave him the glass of water before answering. He drank from it as she spoke. "It is that woman that has called the house asking you for advice about her mother," replied Catherine. "I think her name is Helen?"

Paul tried his best not to act nervous. "What does she want?"

"She wouldn't say," said Catherine.

"I'll see what's the matter," he said while giving her the glass. He grabbed the robe at the bottom of the bed and ran downstairs, knotting it in the middle.

"Did she go through with it?" wondered Paul while lifting the receiver.

"Helen?" asked Paul while stretching the long phone cord into the study so Catherine wouldn't hear.

"Is that you, Paul?" asked Helen while almost whispering.

"Yes, Helen, it's me. What's going on?" entreated Paul.

"I haven't seen or heard from you in weeks," said Helen.

"Helen, now is not the time for," Paul started.

Helen interrupted, "my mother is dead, Paul. The Police are here. There are two officers in her room as we speak. They are requesting you come to the house and make the pronouncement. Otherwise, they would have to call the Rock County Coroner."

Paul's eyelids flickered rapidly. It happened every time he felt he was going to have a panic attack. He thought he had no choice but to go to her. "I'll be there as soon as I can."

"Good," said Helen. "Very good," she said before hanging up.

Paul stood there, flabbergasted.

"Did she do it?" he asked himself.

"Do what?" asked Catherine, now behind him.

"Jesus! Don't do that! You almost gave me a heart attack, woman!" exclaimed Paul.

"What did she want at this hour?" asked Catherine while opening the refrigerator to grab the milk.

"Her mother passed away. I have to go and make the pronouncement," said Paul wondering how he would handle the encounter once he got there.

"I'm sorry to hear. How long will you be gone?" Catherine asked while drinking milk.

"Not long, I hope," he replied.

Paul went upstairs and gathered pants and a shirt from his closet.

"I always thought her calling you here at the house was sort of strange," started Catherine. "She was the only one of your patients that did so. I don't want to sound insensitive, but to be honest, I'm glad that won't be happening anymore."

"Her mother was very ill," said Paul while buttoning his shirt. "Try to show a little compassion."

Paul had not given Helen his home number. She had tricked his young and inexperienced secretary by pretending to be an old schoolmate contacting him for a school reunion.

"Don't forget your belt," said Catherine while passing it to him.

"Okay, thanks. I'll be back soon," said Paul, now tightening his shoes.

"Okay," replied Catherine.

* * *

When Paul met Helen, she instantly captivated him. Her eyes spoke of a vulnerability he felt a need to protect. Her blonde-reddish hair flowed like the unstoppable passion of hot lava down the necked slope he desired to kiss. Her lips smiled, often flirting a great deal without much effort.

Paul liked that Helen was playful and always had time to listen. She frequently complimented him on his good looks and loved it when he wore suits. It had become a ritual that she combed his hair always before he left. It had been somewhat awkward the first time she did, but now Paul had grown accustomed to it and desired the farewell treatment. Gradually he noticed he found himself wanting to spend more time around her.

His friendship with Helen had evolved from silent flirting to one full of sexual tension. With Helen's every smile, move and look, Paul felt himself drifting into carelessness for his marriage.

The affair started unintended. It didn't take long for it to escalate to the point where Paul thought *"the hell with it"* and grabbed her one day, throwing her on the dining room table. He threw the flower vase to the floor, making it shatter when it hit the ground. He raised her sundress above her waist.

"I have been waiting for this moment for a long time Paul," she said.

Paul made passionate love to Helen that night and into the morning.

The fight he had with Catherine the prior evening about his long hours at work helped him conceal his whereabouts. He told her he had stayed at a hotel that night.

Paul found himself finding excuses to visit Helen at every chance he could. He defined their lovemaking as something *out of this world.* There was no doubt he was falling for Helen.

The last time Paul had seen Helen, she had asked to speak to him in private. She led him to the living room and asked him to sit, "I thought you should know my mom is starting to become suspicious of our relationship and is asking lots of questions."

"Really?" asked Paul reluctantly, "how could she notice? She never comes out of that dark bedroom."

Helen ignored his comment and continued, "It has been six months since we started this thing, Paul. I don't even know what to call it. Don't you think it is time for us to move to the next level and truly be together?"

"Together? Paul tried to conceal his shock. "But your mother..."

"My mother, Paul?" Helen asked, sounding irritated, "what about my mother?" she continued without waiting for an answer, "the better-suited question would be; what about your wife? I thought we would talk about your divorce first."

Paul was surprised Helen mentioned the word divorce, "do not be concerned with my marriage. Divorce is only a matter of legalities," he said, "your situation is more complex and requires creative ingenuity."

"What do you mean?" asked Helen.

"Listen," he said, moving forward on the chair, "everyone in town believes your mother is very sick," Helen nodded, "we'll just overdose her with medication," he laughed. "Problem solved," he finished jokingly.

"Will that kill her instantly?"

Paul was dumbfounded. It was not a proposition, only a joke. A sick one nonetheless but a joke regardless.

"I don't know Helen. It is highly possible, but I'm not completely sure," replied Paul.

"Good," said Helen.

"There is no way you could get away with it," said Paul to a skeptical Helen. "If something were to happen to your mother, the coroner would find out easily anyway," he said, trying to scare her into dismissing the idea.

"Would he, Paul? Not with your help, they wouldn't."

Paul decided it was better to remain silent. The conversation had turned uncomfortable. It was time to leave.

"It has to be quick and clean," Helen said, sounding determined.

"You should reconsider, Helen," Paul said. "Think about the seriousness of what you are saying. Don't do anything rash."

"Do you want us to be together, Paul?" asked Helen, looking straight into his eyes. "The answer is easy: Yes, or no?"

Paul hesitated. Things seemed to be spiraling out of control. Sure, she was attractive, and the secrecy of their romance had been exhilarating. But he had never intended for things to go dark. He had had multiple affairs, but nothing had prepared him for this type of psychopathic relationship.

"Paul?" insisted Helen.

"Yes, the answer is yes!" Paul lied. "But I think we should wait," Paul replied.

"Nonsense," blurted Helen.

"Okay then, there's my cue," said Paul while standing and grabbing the car keys. "It is time for me to go. Your mom could probably hear us, you know. She's just a few steps away in the other room."

"Is that it?" asked Helen, sounding argumentative, "that's the end of the conversation? Won't you even give it a second thought?"

"This is crazy," said Paul while walking towards the door.

She followed. "It seems nothing will change your mind. Will it?" Paul asked her before opening the door.

"Nope," replied Helen.

"Do you want to be with me that badly?" asked

the doctor.

"You know I do," Helen replied, "very much so," she said.

Paul had regretted what he said after. Strangely enough, part of him wanted her to do it. And honestly, he would've been okay with it if so much wasn't at stake.

"Then you know what you have to do," said Paul. "I don't want to know the details. Just do it and make it look natural. I'll take care of the rest." He told her what he thought she wanted to hear. Mostly, he hated conflict and prevented having a scene outside. He was sure she would not follow through with the idea. Helen was not the killer type. No way.

Helen nodded reflectively while Paul opened the door. She kissed him on the cheek, "don't you worry about a thing, my love. I'm glad you have helped me decide. I needed that push. I know what I have to do now."

"Please, Helen, you can't take what I've just told you seriously. I didn't mean what I said," pleaded Paul.

Helen pursed her lips and closed the door behind him. Paul stood at the doorway. What she had just said worried him much. She was considering murder.

IV THE CRIME SCENE

Felonies were almost nonexistent in Edom. A murder happened "once in a blue moon." That made people, differently from the metropolis, be easily scandalized when anything occurred.

The Chief of Police, Carl Swanson, worked obsessively to keep out controversies. Mainly for a couple of reasons, he wanted to ride out quietly his last years before retirement and hated any bad press. Carlson had been the Chief for the last twenty-five years.

The Chief defined himself as a "spirit of the law" kind of guy. Some of his subordinates disagreed with his halfhearted views on the enforcement of the law. Detective Aldie was one of them. He didn't hide it.

The phone rang late at night. The Chief knew what it meant. When Carlson heard Aldie's voice, his blood pressure instantly went up.

"What now, Aldie?" asked the Chief. "Must be bad news. Otherwise, you wouldn't be bothering me this late at night. Would you now, Aldie?"

"No, Chief. I wouldn't," said Aldie. "I have a dead body."

"Who is it, Aldie?" asked the Chief annoyingly.

"It's Elizabeth Baron."

"Baron? Isn't she the woman who wouldn't come out of her house?"

"Yep, that's the one."

"Goddamn it, Aldie, what makes you think her death is suspicious?"

"I don't know, Chief. Gut instinct, I guess. The body's position on the bed doesn't match someone dying of choking on food."

"I'm not tracking."

"You'd think a person would stand up. Put up a fight to survive, you know? And her daughter's story doesn't jive. The whole thing appears strange."

"Okay, now you are putting your spin on it like you always do. It sounds like you want to make a mountain out of a molehill."

"I don't think," Aldie stopped when the Chief took a deep breath.

"Damn it, Aldie. I don't need this," said the Chief. "We can't have the town worried and scared."

"None of us want that, Chief," said Aldie in a condescending tone.

"Excuse me?"

"Never mind."

"Who is the treating physician?"

Aldie found it odd the Chief did not know it was Paul as he was friendly with the Thomas Family.

"It is Dr. Thomas. Dr. Paul Thomas."

"The good old doctor, eh"?

"Oh lord, here we go," thought Aldie.

Aldie was afraid that would happen. He guessed Chief Carlson would use the doctor as an excuse not to investigate further.

"Hell, Aldie, in that case, why the hell did you wake me up? Have the good old doctor pronounce her dead and move on. Don't go making things more difficult for the rest of us. If the doctor says there is no suspicious death, then there's no suspicious death. Comprende?"

"Okay, Okay," replied Aldie. Now Helen was standing next to him.

"By the way, how's that sister of mine doing? I have to give her a call one of these days."

"Mom is fine. I must go now. The daughter of the deceased is standing next to me. She may have some additional information," said Aldie looking at Helen in the eyes.

The Chief took Aldie's tone as an indication he would investigate further. "Hold on for a minute. I want to make one thing clear."

"And what's that?"

"I know how you like to question authority, nephew. You've always done it. On this one, please listen to the doctor. I hate to repeat myself but pay attention. If he says it was a natural death, don't be chasing trouble, you hear?

"Uh-huh, sure."

"And also, please offer my condolences to the daughter."

"Will do. Goodbye."

The phone clicked back in place, and Aldie turned to Helen.

* * *

Paul wondered how many cops would be at the house. He imagined himself behind bars. He thought about a criminal conviction and his job. He played in his head what his colleagues at the hospital would say if everything came out in the open. They would be highly disappointed. The program he developed would not even make any budget talks next year. He should've cared more about the consequences before he got involved with Helen.

The Medical Board of trustees at Rock Hospital entrusted him two years ago to develop the home-visit program for low-income patients. The goal was to care for people at their homes who did not have the financial resources to stay at the hospital long-term. It was a resuscitation of the old community doctor program, caring for patients at their homes. Most of these patients had relatives that provided 24/7 care to them. Helen was one of those.

Paul was getting closer to Helen's house and dreaded it. He tried to guess some of the questions he would face by the police and asked them out loud.

"What is Elizabeth Baron's illness? How long have you known her daughter? Have you slept with her?"

Paul became anxious. He couldn't take his mind

off a possible murder conviction and jail. He wondered what Helen's life would be like now that her mother was no longer alive. He imagined her in the house, alone, wearing the same sundress while having coffee at the table, happy about the outcome.

Paul noticed for the first time he had not visualized himself in the same room with her. It didn't bother him, and he was glad he wasn't. He had concluded Helen was bad news.

Helen's house came to view like a horror house where only the crazy would venture in.

Paul stopped and turned off the engine. He looked at the entrance. He was back at the place a lot sooner than he would've liked. It was an unfamiliar scene to see an ambulance parked in front, and two marked Police cruisers on the driveway.

Paul took a deep breath and reached into the black bag to grab the stethoscope.

It started to drizzle, and Paul ran to the house.

✳ ✳ ✳

An officer came into the room and made a gesture. "Another car just arrived. It is a fancy one. I think the doctor just got here," he said.

"We must go and meet him now.," said Helen, trying her best not to sound excited.

"I know. But before we go to talk to the doctor, can I ask you a few more questions?"

"Why? I have been cooperative so far," replied Helen coldly.

Helen looked at the detective. She thought he wasn't an attractive man by any means. He was grossly overweight, and his face showed lunar scars left by years of untreated aggressive acne.

"Please try to make it short, detective," said Helen trying to read what Aldie was jotting down on his pocket notebook, "this is hard enough already."

Detective Aldie had been a detective for most of his Law Enforcement career. Most of his colleagues avoided him. He was the chief's nephew, and that made them uncomfortable. They believed they wouldn't be able to speak freely without their conversation finding its way up to the top man. They thought he was arrogant.

Aldie had isolated himself because of the mistrust he felt around him. His peers had interpreted his behavior as having a chip on his shoulder. Nothing was further from the truth. Aldie was not the mole his colleagues made him out to be. Like them, he also avoided his uncle at all costs.

Chief Carlson had always been critical of Aldie. He didn't like his propensity to question everything.

"There you go again, nephew, asking questions," would often say the Chief. "When are you going to learn that some things are just better left alone? No need to understand everything. You'll drive yourself crazy."

* * *

Paul stopped at the front door and shook his shoes to remove the mud. He looked at the Police cruiser parked in front of the house and heard a muffled voice on its radio spitting words and codes he could not understand.

He approached the front door raising his fist and knocking softly. A uniformed cop who did not look older than twenty-one opened it.

"You must be...?" said the young officer.

"I am Doctor Paul Thomas. I was summoned here for the pronouncement." Paul was relieved the officer did not appear experienced.

"Oh yes, please come on in! We have been expecting you," said the officer excitedly. Now that the doctor had arrived, he didn't have to stand guard over the dead body any longer.

The Officer asked Paul how to spell his name and scribbled it on a notepad that showed several names already. "Please proceed to the kitchen. They are expecting you."

The house was quiet without the usual sounds of the oldies playing in the background. Paul's hands became sweaty, and his heart rate doubled, "good thing I am not about to take a Polygraph test," he thought.

He walked towards the kitchen and took a deep breath.

"Game face on," Paul thought.

He pushed open the door that was half ajar.

* * *

"I'm sorry, Ms. Baron. I know this is not pleasant in any shape or form," said Aldie.

Helen did not want to answer any more questions. She had already told Aldie the story as she had rehearsed it many times. She was afraid to say something that would incriminate her.

"Miss Baron, can I see the bowl?" Asked Aldie.

"What bowl?"

"You said earlier that you were feeding your mother oatmeal out of the bowl before she passed. I couldn't find it in the bedroom. Where is it?"

"I washed it," replied Helen.

"And why would you..." started the Detective.

The door to the room opened. Both the Detective and Helen turned.

"Who's in charge here?" asked Paul, entering the kitchen abrasively.

"Paul! I'm so glad you are finally here!" exclaimed

Helen while running to his arms.

"Save me," she whispered in his ear. Then loudly, "These cops are making me feel like a criminal!"

Aldie frowned. He stood a few seconds before approaching.

Paul felt uncomfortable and did not embrace Helen. He thought, "not here, not now," he tried to push her softly away from him. She resisted.

"Doctor Thomas?" said Aldie while stretching out his hand. "The infamous doctor Thomas?" Aldie smirked. "Nice to meet you. I'm Detective Aldie. John Aldie."

"Infamous?" said Paul while stretching his hand behind Helen. He hoped Aldie's comment didn't imply that Helen had been saying things she shouldn't.

"Just a joke, doctor. A little police humor, that's all," replied the Detective, now showing a serious face, "I can say on behalf of all of us that we are glad you are finally here. As you are aware, we cannot move the body until you make the pronouncement."

"Yes, of course. I understand," said Paul, placing the stethoscope in his ears, "Can anyone give me a general idea of what happened?" asked Paul, trying to sound as if the question was a matter of only straight professionalism. His true intent was to assess the threat level to his freedom.

"If you don't mind, can we attend to that in a few minutes? I'll be right with you," said Aldie. "I was about to ask Ms. Baron a few more questions."

"I don't want to sound rude, Detective," said Paul. "But I must get back to my family," he said while looking at Helen. "It is late."

"Hmm, we can't have Doctor Thomas wait now, can we?" said Aldie while closing his notebook. "Right, Ms. Baron?" he finished sarcastically.

Aldie noticed the way Helen was staring at the doctor. Her stare was lustful and reckless. Like she didn't care that anyone knew her feelings. That raised his suspicions that Elizabeth's death had not been accidental.

"This way, please," Helen pointed.

The doctor went, and Aldie followed.

❊ ❊ ❊

Elizabeth had been covered with a white sheet by a young officer.

"Who covered her?" Asked Aldie, now turning to the two uniformed officers behind him.

The young officer raised his hand cowardly.

"I know you are a rookie, but this is unacceptable," said Aldie angrily. "Preserve the crime scene at all costs! Do you understand me? That means not changing anything without asking someone first!"

"Hold on, hold on since when is this a crime scene?" said Helen.

Paul interjected, "calm down, Helen. The Detective is trying to do his job. Once I make the death pronouncement, I'm sure we can all return to doing better things. Right Detective?"

Paul didn't want to bring negative attention to Helen or himself if Helen started questioning the Police. Paul looked at the Detective for affirmation.

"It looks like you two are on a first-name basis," Aldie said while pointing at them, making a two with his right index and middle fingers.

Paul took a step forward. "Not sure what you're insinuating, Detective. I have been taking care of her mother for some time now. It makes things a lot easier in my profession when both patient and caretaker can trust their doctor."

"Very well. Let's get to it, shall we?" said Aldie while uncovering Elizabeth.

The doctor went to Elizabeth and put the stethoscope on her exposed back, listening for any sign of a heartbeat. Paul looked at his Rolex and said, "Death pronouncement date is April 10th, 1970, with an official time of 11:53 PM."

Aldie wrote the time down on his notepad. "Thank you, doctor. Can I ask you a few routine questions?"

"There seems to be nothing routine about your questions, Detective," said Paul.

Aldie displayed a smirk. He turned to the three officers standing in the room. "One of you, please call the funeral home on your way out. The owners live there on the premises so you should find someone at this hour without a problem. You," said Aldie pointing to the younger officer, "you will stay and wait for the funeral home to arrive." The officer understood that was his punishment for tampering with the scene. "Please cover her back up," finished Aldie.

"With me, doctor," said Aldie, walking toward the front door. Helen followed. The Detective stopped and looked at Helen with curiosity.

Helen frowned.

"Helen, would you be a dear and make us a cup of coffee?" asked Paul, hoping Helen would comply without protest.

Both Paul and Detective Aldie stepped into the living room.

"I'm a man that doesn't like to mince words, doctor, so I'm just going to come out and say it, are you having a romantic relationship with Ms. Baron?"

"What?"

"She hasn't taken her eyes off you since you came in, doctor," said Aldie, now taking out a cigarette.

"Can you please not?" asked Paul.

Aldie put the cigarette away in his chest pocket.

"I'm not sure where this line of questioning is going, but I don't like it," said Paul.

"My apologies, doctor. I don't mean to offend. I wouldn't be doing my job if I didn't explore the possibilities. You never know," he finished.

"I don't care much for your insinuations, Detective. They seem to be justifications for being inappropriate," said Paul. "Now, I'd like to head home if you don't mind?"

"What was the disease she suffered from again?"

"She suffered from Cardiomyopathy, but for those that did not go to medical school, it is another name for a weak heart. But I don't think that's what killed her."

"Oh?"

"Don't get excited, Detective. She was not a healthy woman. I guess that she most likely suffered a heart attack."

"Really? Miss Baron said she choked."

"Some people may manifest similar symptoms when having a heart attack," said Paul. "Asphyxia-induced cardiac arrest can occur if there is airway obstruction like choking on food, for example. I wouldn't pay much attention to her statements, Detective. I'm sure Helen is under much duress. She loved her mother very much."

Helen appeared with a wooden tray holding two cups of black coffee.

"Thank you, Miss Baron, but I must leave now," said Aldie while taking a cigarette out of his pocket and lighting it. "You may want to stay here and have your coffee, doctor," he said while looking at Helen. "I'm a tea man myself. I'm sure there are many things you both need to talk about."

Aldie walked out and started walking toward his car. An older officer appeared behind him, tipped his hat as if saying goodbye, and walked to his patrol vehicle, the furthest car away from the house.

Paul walked to the porch, and Helen followed. "Paul?" she called. He stopped, and Helen put the tray on the ground. One of the coffee cups spilled. She ignored it.

"Don't start with me, Helen. I know what you are going to say."

"Do you, Paul? Because honestly, I don't think you do."

"You are going to ask me why I disappeared. I'm sorry, I've been busy. A lot of people depend on me."

"No need to explain. It's pretty apparent," Helen

said. Then continued, "you are trying to break up with me, and you think that avoiding me is the way to do it. But what you don't understand is that I get the message. I heard you loud and clear; you lied to me. You are not leaving your wife, as you promised."

"Listen," started Paul. "Don't be dramatic. I just helped you here."

"No, Paul. You helped only yourself," said Helen while taking the recorder out of her pocket. She pressed the play button, and the wheels turned like those on a patty wagon. "Just make it look natural," his voice on the recorder.

"How could you?" asked Paul, enraged. "No one will believe you."

"They won't? It's your voice and what you say here makes you an accomplice. Don't try to be a hero, and you won't have any problems. I promise," Helen said. "Don't ever contact me again."

Helen grabbed the tray and walked inside the house, closing the door behind her.

Paul stood there, all becoming crystal clear; Helen had shown her cards, and he had lost.

V MY MOTHER'S GRAVE

The Indiangrass on the ridge's side moved in unison in one direction, then suddenly to another like a bird murmuration. Their golden-yellow plumes shone like poor man's gold blowing away in the wind.

It was another hot day, yet the wind brought needed relief. Helen looked at the sky. The few cumulus clouds absent of heavy water made it look free of inclement weather.

It was her mother's two-month death anniversary. She failed to visit the grave on the first one. The breakup with Paul hit her harder emotionally than she anticipated. Her grief was sometimes too much to bear.

For the last several weeks, she had done nothing but thought of ways to get revenge. She wanted so many times to call, even to harass Paul in person at home. To be the type of woman who proudly appears on the newspaper's front page for burning her lover's house down. That would've felt good; she could savor it. Her pregnancy and unwanted police attention had stopped her from executing her impulses.

To add to her distress, Detective Aldie had been relentless. He seemed to be a very intuitive man, like most cops, she assumed. They seem to be experts at uncovering hidden guilt. Or is it that maybe like her, their guilt couldn't stop them from appearing insecure about lies told? She felt very vulnerable around him. She thought of herself as a tough woman immune to intimidation. Resilient. A free thinker with no qualms about stirring the pot whenever necessary.

Helen had seen Aldie outside her window, interviewing Carmen and snooping around. The detective stopped by the house unannounced on several occasions to question her. Helen couldn't recall if it were six or seven times. More than five, for sure. His inquiries never ceased to feel like bear traps, carefully dropped in sinister conversational places waiting for her to step on one of them neglectfully. He would ask a question; then, a few minutes later, ask it again differently.

Helen had received good news; the County Coroner denied the detective's petition for an autopsy of Elizabeth's body. The coroner described a profound lack of evidence combined with Doctor Thomas's well-written statement and official death pronouncement as reasons for the rejection.

In one of his unexpected visits, Aldie sounded resentful while telling the story. Helen wondered about his motivation to relay such failure. She guessed it was his way of telling her, "no matter, I'll catch you regardless." There was a slight chance he was using it like some weird psychological warfare tactic to break her down and make her give up. She felt his ultimate goal was to get her to confess right there on her front porch. It would be a hell of a lot easier than dragging her into the station under a hunch pretense and having to explain himself to his superiors.

Helen worried about what made Aldie suspect her in such an obstinate way. What, if any, clues did the detective possess? The thought of Aldie finding out what she had done terrified her.

She used anger to try to deter the detective. It had been a waste of time. She gradually became meaner and essentially very uncooperative. Helen became so fearful she would slip during one interaction that she decided to stop the intrusions.

Not soon after Aldie left her doorstep, Helen decided to call Chief Carlson and make a formal complaint. She told the Chief that the detective had been at her house several times harassing her and using intimidation tactics to get her to admit to a crime she did not commit.

Carlson expressed utter dismay and outrage. He apologized and assured her he didn't know anything about it. He promised he would follow up and told her not to worry any longer; Aldie wouldn't be by her house ever again.

* * *

The cemetery was less than a mile away. Helen decided to walk. "The exercise would do me right," she told herself.

No sooner did Helen start walking; sweat ran down her forehead. She grabbed a tissue from her bulky black leather purse and wiped her brow. Helen thought it would be wise to go back and get her car, but she had already been walking for a few minutes. She distracted herself by thinking of her baby.

The pregnancy had been a welcomed surprise. How long had it been? Good thing she wasn't showing. She needed time to prepare a response to the main question: "Who's the father?"

She worried she would need to go to the hospital sooner rather than later for a check-up. An examination was the logical thing to do. Helen had resisted; the medical staff would undoubtedly ask lots of personal questions.

Helen's yellow sundress flew slightly upwards with the wind. She heard the wooden heels making staccato sounds that made her painfully aware of the distance gone and the one still to come. The walk to the cemetery became one of those good ideas that quickly turned into regret. Helen classified walking the mile as another wrong decision to throw in the "bad decisions" jar if there was one. This one would've been the tiny drop that overfilled the jar. There was not one car in sight and no sign of drinkable water. The summer heat from the road was coming upwards like flames in a grill.

A few minutes later, like a mirage, the cemetery sign showed in the distance. The heat haze made the letters distorted and creepy. Helen had been by it a million times. She knew the rusted steel sign read, "Cemetery of Edom."

Helen stepped up her pace. The sky turned suddenly ominous to the northwest. Storms often came and went in North Carolina summers like unannounced guests. The dark gray and dense clouds looked unwelcoming, seemingly anxious to drop their water weight. If she were to avoid the rain, she had to do her chore and get back to the house.

Helen took shade from the unforgiving sun under the tall weeping willow tree at the cemetery entrance. The temperature was cooler under it. It felt twenty degrees better.

Summer was her favorite time of year; it was warm, of course. That was the first reason. Secondly, she despised winter. Third, she liked the sudden and robust thunderstorms that appeared to come out of nowhere during summer. The unpredictability of unforeseen chaos and the roaring of thunder felt adventurous and soothing for some inexplicable reason.

There was still some distance to the grave. Helen looked around for a place with some water to offer. She noticed a nearby building that looked like the cemetery office.

A sweaty older man wearing a dirty white shirt was sitting behind a desk. His legs were on it, and he was reading the Edom Gazette. Helen recognized the paper at first sight.

"Would you be so kind as to give this old lady a glass of water? It is hot today, and as you can see, I'm sweating like a sinner in church," Helen said while pushing air to her face with her right hand.

The man put the paper down, revealing a long brown beard. He looked at Helen up and down." Of course, ma'am! With one condition," he replied.

"What's that?"

"That you don't call yourself old. You got more style than Carter's got little pills," said the man winking and smiling while disappearing behind a door.

Helen looked at the calendar on the wall full of squares and small numbers behind the desk. It had names written in black ink made by someone with awful penmanship. The board had ink traces as if it had been erased and written over many times. The July weekends were pretty full. It showed at least one burial for every weekday and three for each Saturday and Sunday. It surprised Helen so many people died in such a small town. Thirty-five people were getting buried that month.

The man returned with a red plastic cup. She

drank the water almost desperately. "Oh, hold down there, miss, slow down," he said jokingly. "We don't want you choking on it. I don't know CPR."

Helen smiled while placing the cup on the counter.

"Would you like another one?"

"No, thank you."

"So, I assume you are on your way to a grave?"

"Yeah."

"Which one? Maybe I can help?"

"No worries. It is my mother's. I have a pretty good idea where it is."

"I reckon I haven't seen you around these parts before. Is it a fresh grave?"

"I'm sorry?" asked Helen, confused by the" fresh grave" term. She found it insensitive.

"My apologies. Us gravediggers are often guilty of forgetting how to talk to the living folk properly," said the man." How long has it been since the funeral?"

"Three months to the date."

"My condolences. What's her last name?"

"It is Baron, Elizabeth Baron."

"Oh, okay. I know that site well. I was there this morning," said the man." Listen, I want to apologize in advance."

"For what?"

"Your mom's grave is on a downhill slope. During the last torrential rain a few weeks ago, everything washed away on your mother's grave to include the flowers and temporary marker," he said, worried about Helen's reaction. " You see, it's only me, myself, and I who's doing all of the hard labor around here until we hire someone else. I've been so busy I haven't had time to fix it."

"But you have time to read the paper while having your feet up," thought Helen.

"I can drive you," the man offered while grabbing a set of keys hanging on the wall. "I'm Don, by the way."

"No, thank you, Don," said Helen without purposely giving out her name.

"Okay, then. Suit yourself," Don said while grabbing the newspaper and sitting back down. He put his legs on the table. "When you get down there, if you are not sure of the grave, you'll know it'll be your mom's plot because it is next to another one covered with flowers," the gravedigger said." It is the grave of a young person we buried yesterday. Very sad."

"Okay," said Helen." Bye."

Don noticed Helen seemed bothered by him and decided not to engage her any longer even though he had felt like asking her out on a date. At his age, chances for romance were next to none in Edom. Everyone seemed to be married or unavailable. He noticed she had no rings on her left hand.

Helen exited, walking by many graves along the way. The cemetery looked crowded. She looked at the tombstones and read the years people died. Helen liked to imagine how they lived. The older the headstone, the better. There was one that read that the person's year of death was 1912. She imagined how rural the town would've been in that year with dirt roads and farms everywhere. Probably not even cars in town then.

She walked by an older black couple that was sitting quietly, staring at a headstone. Helen could see the headstone's first name read "Diana." Most likely their daughter. She decided not to disturb them and proceeded forward. About twenty feet away, she could see the grave the gravedigger had described full of flowers.

Helen stopped at her mother's grave that looked worse than she thought. It was a patch of bare dirt with almost no signs a burial had taken place if not for the slight depression in the middle.

The dry streaks where the water had traveled were still there. The gravedigger did not exaggerate; the rain had ravaged the burial site. She shook her head in disbelief and sat on the ground.

She stretched the skirt of her dress, her legs under it, and looked down at the grave. "Sorry, not sorry, mother," Helen started. "I came to tell you that I think you deserved what I did to you and to let you know I'm never coming back here," she finished while grabbing some dirt.

Helen looked back at the couple she had passed. The woman was now resting on the man's shoulder. He seemed to be consoling her.

The leaves chatting with the wind stopped suddenly. Silence reigned. Curiously, Helen looked up at the tall trees. Their canopy colored much of the sky with its lush greenery. A mix of dark gray nimbus clouds, sun rays, and blue sky injected themselves in the above opening.

Helen looked down at the grave. A sudden deep red mist emanated from it, shaping into the sil-

houette of a woman. The figure showed a youthful Elizabeth. Helen remembered her mother's
face from old photos.

She stood, not knowing what to do. "Mother?"

Her mother's face smiled eerily, staring at Helen
straight in the eye. Helen was about to speak
again when the mist flew into her nose, inserting itself into Helen's body with her next breath.
Helen took a step back in shock and disbelief."
I'm just confused. The heat is making me see
things," she thought.

Helen was about to turn and leave when she felt
an acute pain in her abdomen. She grabbed her
waist and let out a deep breath failing miserably
at making the pain go away. It became intolerable. She fell to the ground. Her hands, now on
her belly, started to feel movement inside of her.
Her belly started growing like a balloon. She let
out a loud and painful yell making the old couple
rush to her.

It began to rain hard.

The woman knelt next to Helen and looked at her
belly.

Helen's dress had ripped around her waist

to make space for the unexpected mass. She showed a full pregnancy.

"Darnell, this woman is about to give birth. Hurry, go get the car!" she said.

The rain intensified. Helen was in such agony she was unaware of the drenching. Her contractions were too painful to witness anything else. "It looks like you are in active labor, my dear," said the woman. "Lucky for you, I'm a retired nurse."

The pain felt excruciating. "Active labor?" Helen thought. "How's this possible? Am I having a miscarriage?" she started to hyperventilate.

The car brakes squealed, bringing the vehicle abruptly to a stop on the muddy road, making it slip slightly forward. Darnell exited and ran to Helen and his wife.

"Help me lift her, honey," the woman said.

Both lifted Helen by the shoulders and helped her to the back seat of the Ford Squire Wagon. Helen moaned.

The car sped, making its way out of the cemetery. The wipers were now ejecting water off of the windshield left to right at full force.

Helen was now mumbling. She was sweating profusely and was delirious. She kept repeating, "vita in morte sumus."

"She's saying some weird stuff," the woman said. "That's not good," She looked at her husband in the front seat." Darnell, I know it is raining hard out here, and I hate to ask you this, but we must hurry and get to Rock Hospital as soon as we can."

"Okay, I'll do my best," he responded.

Helen drifted. Her mother's murder playing like an awful reminder of what she had

VI THE EARLY BIRD

The hospital's parking lot was nearly empty. Darnell and Jasmine grabbed Helen and entered the emergency room.

"Please," pleaded Jasmine to the triage nurse. "This woman seems to be in labor. She has been hyperventilating and has gone out of consciousness several times on the way here. It would be best if you got her in right away."

"Jeff, please come here!" yelled the nurse to a man dressed in blue scrubs some distance away. "And bring a wheelchair."

The nurse grabbed the wheelchair and sat Helen on it.

"I'm a retired nurse," Jasmine told them. "I must tell you that she seemed to be having contractions when we found her, and her water broke on the way here."

"Are you related?" asked the female nurse. Jasmine shook her head.

"Friends of hers?"

The male nurse pushed the wheelchair through a set of doors that read "Authorized Personnel Only."

"No, we brought her here from the cemetery," replied Jasmine.

"The cemetery?" asked the nurse while frowning.

"The woman seemed to be visiting someone's grave just like we were. She was near us when we heard her yell for help."

"Thank you. You are both welcome to stay, but it is not necessary, and it may be a long while," said the nurse before disappearing through the doors.

※ ※ ※

A female doctor appeared next to Helen and asked the nurses to lay her down in an empty bed.

"Okay, okay, stay with me," said the doctor, noticing Helen was breathing intensely.

"You are safe now. We will take care of you," she

told Helen while examining her pupils with a penlight. "Your breathing may be problematic for us later if it keeps going at this rate," she said. "How long have you been pregnant?"

"I don't know. Two months or so, I guess," replied Helen.

"Okay, interesting. Based on the size of your abdomen, you seem to be having a full-term pregnancy," said the doctor while taking her temperature. "She's apyrexial. No high temperature, so that's good."

"Who's your doctor?" asked Doctor Chen to Helen.

"I don't have one," Helen said, letting out a big exhale to ease the pain.

The doctor decided not to ask Helen any more questions and turned to the female nurse.

"Okay, it seems we are on our own on this one without any antenatal nor medical history. It looks to me like the patient is showing 40 weeks' gestation. The abdomen shows a full-term pregnancy. Her cervix dilation is contracting every 5 to ten minutes now. The patient seems mildly dehydrated."

The female nurse nodded, "Doctor?"

"Yeah, what?"

"I thought you should know, the couple that brought her here is not related to her. They happened to be at the same place she was. The woman told us she was a retired nurse and said our patient was hyperventilating. She also said she was drifting in and out of consciousness."

"Got it," said the doctor, turning to Helen. "Her pupils react to light, her reflexes are normal, her heart rate is 77 beats per minute, her cervix is about 7 cm dilated. The patient is tachypnoeic. Let's try the Ambu bag."

"Already on it," replied the male nurse reaching for the cabinet.

The nurse applied the bag valve mask to Helen's face and started squeezing gently. Helen's breathing started normalizing after a few repetitions.

"Good," said the doctor.

"Let's go ahead and start lab tests, and once you are able, obtain consent for extradural analgesia," said the doctor before going to see another patient across the way.

* * *

Helen was woken by a nurse shaking her shoulder.

"How are you feeling?" asked the nurse.

Helen looked up. The nurse standing in front of her was young with a gentle face.

"Sore."

"The doctor will be by later, but first, I wanted to congratulate you on your healthy baby boy."

"A baby? What, baby?"

"Yes, a healthy baby boy. He came into this world, weighing almost 6 pounds, 5.8 to be exact," the nurse said while lifting the bed a little higher. "That weight is a little on the lower end, but we are watching him now. I'm sure he'll be fine."

"A baby?" Helen asked. "I don't understand. This is not supposed to be happening."

Helen had been pregnant for only a short while. Unless something had moved her biological time clock forward, it was an impossibility.

"The doctor had to perform an emergency C-section. You started hyperventilating after we thought we had your breathing under control," the nurse said while now checking her IV drip." You also became unconscious. It is rare, but it happens."

"Okay," said Helen, very confused.

"Do you have anybody we can call? Maybe the father?"

"No, no, father," said Helen." He's not around. I have no one."

"Well, we have services here that can assist you."

"Yeah, okay, thank you," said Helen.

"I'll be back later. The doctor may be back in a few. Try to rest," said the nurse standing by the opening in the curtain. "If you need anything, please don't hesitate to call us using that red button next to your hand right there." The nurse slid the curtain closed as she exited Helen's space.

"How can this be?" thought Helen. "I did not have a full pregnancy. I wasn't even halfway there. I'm not going crazy; I'm not. There must be something wrong with that baby. Is it even my baby? Are they trying to pawn an unwanted one on me? I'm sure the vision of my younger mother at the cemetery was a hallucination and has nothing to do with it. What's going on?"

The curtain rolled open, and Doctor Chen appeared.

"The nurse is telling me you may have a few questions," said Doctor Chen, arms crossed. She stood at the footboard of the bed. She grabbed the chart and looked at it before continuing, "it is normal to feel confused after coming out of anesthesia. It takes longer for some to fully recover. I am sorry we had to do a C-section. You will be sore for a few weeks."

"You don't get it," said Helen, looking away. "I'm not supposed to be here. I'm not supposed to be having a baby right now."

"Okay, Helen," said the doctor, "is it okay if I call you Helen?"

Helen nodded.

"I was there," the doctor said in a nurturing way. "I performed the procedure. This baby came out of you, and it is a healthy one. If you don't want him, there are programs in," Helen interrupted the doctor. "That's not what I mean," she said while trying to sit up.

"I would advise against getting up right now," said the doctor while she put her hand on Helen's shoulder.

Helen stopped with her chest partially lifted. She rested on her elbows.

"I walked to the cemetery earlier today. While there, something extraordinary happened. I'm still trying to make sense of it."

"Yeah, those friendly people that brought you in told us that's where your contractions started."

"That's the point; I am not supposed to be here having a baby."

The doctor frowned.

"I know you must think there is something wrong with me," said Helen.

The doctor stood there, trying to decide what to say next. In all her years as a doctor, she had heard strange tales but nothing like this. She was at a loss for words.

"Wait a minute," said Helen." Are you trying to give me an abandoned baby? Did I lose mine, and now you are trying to force an orphan on me?"

"I assure you that's not the case," said the doctor sternly. She looked at her watch." I must go and see another patient. There are options out there if you don't want this baby, you know. I'll keep you here for observation for a couple of more days. In the meantime, perhaps another blanket? A pillow?"

"A glass of cold water would be nice."

"I'll ask the nurse to bring it for you. But before I

allow that, I want to make sure there's no bleeding."

"Thank you."

❋ ❋ ❋

Helen woke up the third day in the hospital, excited and anxious to go home. The doctor hadn't
returned after their last conversation a few days
back.

"Hi," greeted the person behind the curtain.
Helen could see the silhouette of a woman. "Can I
come in?"

Without waiting for a response, the woman
opened the curtain.

"I am Mary Dwyer," she said with a southern accent while approaching and stretching out her
hand. "I am with Child Welfare here in Rock
County."

The woman was tall with a beehive hairdo that
screamed the 1960s. She was carrying an over-
packed brown briefcase with tired and distressed
leather showing many hours of use.

She took a notebook out of the briefcase, looked at her watch, and wrote the date and time. "It seems you might be having some skepticism about your newborn. Something about not believing the baby is yours?"

"I don't know where my baby is," Helen said.

"I apologize. The hospital told me they would wait to bring your baby until I spoke with you," said Mary with the blue pen in her mouth.

Helen thought she had to be very careful about what to say next. If she continued claiming the baby was not hers, they would delay her release from the hospital and hold her for observation. They would most likely keep the baby there or pass it along to a foster home until she was fit to care for him. Or worse, take it from her permanently.

There would be no answers at the hospital about what had occurred at the cemetery or anything related to her baby's sudden birth. She would have to seek closure somewhere else.

"I don't remember saying my baby wasn't mine," lied Helen.

"I get it," said the social worker. She took an orange chair and pulled it close to the bed. She sat on it crossing her legs. "Is it okay if I ask you a few more questions?"

"Yeah," said Helen looking outside the window. It was a beautiful day outside. The sky was blue, and she could see pigeons landing on the tops of small buildings.

"Are you feeling sad?" asked Mary.

"No, I feel confused."

"Do you feel like a failure?

"What?" Helen turned her head toward the social worker. "God, no."

"Do you blame yourself lately more than usual?

"I don't blame myself at all," replied Helen defensively.

"Do you feel discouraged about your future?"

"Not sure how to answer that," said Helen, grabbing a cracker from the wooden bed tray in front of her.

"Can you please try?"

"You know how hard society can be on single mothers nowadays. So much is uncertain when trying to raise a baby on your own and with no father in sight. I'll have to figure it out."

"I see; speaking about the father, here's the form

you need to fill to get the baby's birth certificate," said the woman while getting a form out of her briefcase.

"Do I need to name the father?" asked Helen.

"No, it is not necessary. Although I'm sure your son will have many questions in a few years," said Mary while sounding judgmental.

"I'll cross that bridge when I get there," said Helen. Under the baby's name, she wrote, "Michael Baron."

Mary turned the page on her notebook. "Do you still feel your son is not your son? That there is a conspiracy against you?" the social worker crossed her arms.

"All I want to do right this minute is to get my baby and get out of here."

"I can arrange that," said Ms. Dwyer. "The questionnaire requires me to ask you twenty-one questions. As you can tell, I could've asked you all of them. I have lots of it based on my experience, and trust me, and I know a good mother when I see one. I'm almost certain you are one of those. After our brief conversation and your demeanor, I'm satisfied your baby will be in good hands," She continued while writing down some more.

"Thank you," said Helen.

"I will speak to the doctor. I'm sure you and your baby boy will be going home today."

Helen smiled.

VII ZEUS

Four Years Later

Helen could barely move her cart no more than a few inches at a time around the sea of people that surrounded her. She thought she had been waiting in line forever. Her Timex revealed almost 25 minutes had passed. Three people were in front of her with shopping carts overflowing with groceries. The only cashier available at the grocery store moved like molasses.

It was Thanksgiving. It would be a weird one. Helen never thought the uncertainty of national affairs would trickle so profoundly to the local level. Especially in the small town of Edom. People couldn't stop talking about it. An older woman behind Helen proclaimed disbelief at Nixon's helicopter scene after leaving the White House. She asked her husband if he thought Ford would make a good president. He shrugged non-committally.

Michael grabbed the Tampax box and started chewing one of its corners. "No, Michael," Helen said while taking it and placing it in the shopping cart out of his reach. "No touch," she said sternly.

Michael's expressive blue eyes and soft black hair resembled his father's. The town was full of gossip about who his father may be. Helen had grown attuned and desensitized to the whispers and stares.

Michael was short for a four-year-old, and his baby face made him look a few years younger. He would often be confused for a toddler. It also didn't help that he hadn't spoken yet.

He started doing his usual fidgeting, an obvious sign he was getting restless. He let out a loud yelp full of discontent that caught the attention of those around.

"Is your two-year-old boy getting tired?" asked the older woman behind her. The woman looked at Michael with pity, reminiscing when her kids were the same age. Helen smiled, "he's four but yeah, a little. But I tell you, he has been a lot better than I would've been."

Helen would often wonder if Michael someday would be able to speak. She grew accustomed to his guttural sounds and wished he was a normal kid like the rest of his peers. Her patience was growing thin. With every "duh, da, eh," sound Michael gave, she hoped desperately for an intelligible sound.

"It is a matter of time before he says something," she would console herself as clear words would never materialize.

Helen couldn't tell if, out of annoyance or pure unselfishness, a woman approaching the cashier motioned her to take her place in line ahead of her. Helen hesitated. Michael started to hit the cart's handle with his tiny fists. That sealed the decision. She gratefully accepted.

Helen cleared the cashier. She pushed the cart to her car with a big sigh of relief and unloaded the groceries with haste. Michael now slept. She secured him in the car seat.

Helen started the car and waited for some people walking behind to pass. She looked at Michael and wondered what else could she do to enable him to talk, to say something. Helen regretted the constant obsession that consumed her. She learned to understand Michael's requests, delivered mainly by pointing and using the usual guttural sounds.

She took him for a test for expressive and receptive language development. They found nothing Helen didn't already suspect; he showed normal sensory development range but suffered from delayed expressive language. The therapist recommended more tests and firmly advised her to shorten his television time.

"A recent academic study found a direct correlation between time in front of the TV and delay in linguistic development," said the child therapist.

"Okay, I will cut down his Flintstones time," said Helen sarcastically.

"Before you go," started the therapist. "I must ask, is he being discouraged in any way from speaking?"

Helen became instantly irritated, "are you implying I'm abusing my son?" she asked. "How dare you?"

"I didn't mean to offend," said the therapist. "We have to ask. It's just standard procedure."

"It seems you guys think your so-called procedures give you license to be rude," said Helen while picking up Michael from the chair. "We are leaving."

"The audacity!" Helen said aloud while gathering her purse. She had followed all the recommendations to try to accelerate Michael's development: She read to him, had long attempted dialogues that never failed to be exhausting monologues, and even sang. Nothing worked.

✳ ✳ ✳

There was a stampede of cars moving towards the exit. It appeared the multitude of shoppers conspired to leave the parking lot at the same time. Helen started cursing. She looked at the rearview mirror feeling guilty she did it within earshot of Michael.

Michael played with one of her leather gloves. "What if one day," Helen thought, "he bursts into a dialogue? What if he is holding out just waiting for the right moment?"

Helen's facial expression changed to pity. She never ceased to feel responsible for Michael's shortcomings. Her stress caused Michael's premature birth, not some weird ghostly event.

"I was nine months pregnant, not three, you idiot," she kept telling herself the last four years. Her mother's sudden death, the police questioning that followed, and Paul's abandonment had indeed been stressful factors. She could have been the poster child for "trifecta victimization" if there had been such a thing.

The ghost of her mother at the cemetery, she was sure now, had been a hallucination caused by stress. Yet, she struggled to erase the other-worldly experience out of her mind.

❊ ❊ ❊

The drive home was rather pleasant. Helen turned the radio to her favorite oldies station. She started dancing in the car, her long red hair flying from side to side. An Ad about the grand opening of the Train Station Diner made her think about dinner. Helen began to plan for the turkey, calculating its time to cook and the lovely time with Michael. Helen pressed the accelerator going well above the posted speed limit of 55mph.

"Good thing I decided this morning to go grocery shopping," she thought. A sense of accomplishment invaded her. She procrastinated for a few weeks. Her fears about not finding a turkey on Thanksgiving Day were unfounded. There were plenty of turkeys on sale.

The highway disappeared behind them, turning into a narrow two-lane road that led them to a one-way street. Helen became curious when she drove by the "for sale" signs in several houses' front yards. It came as a surprise. People in her neighborhood usually didn't move out. She could not fault them; newspaper reports named a recent rise in kidney cancer deaths to a "more than acceptable and long-ignored lead level" content in the local potable water.

The community meeting about the lead problem had not gone great for the mayor. It started peacefully. He accepted the blame for the mishap, and people applauded.

Later, the meeting turned nasty when he explained the old infrastructure needed replacing, and to get it done, he would propose to the Town Board an increase in taxes from 5% to 9%. People got angry. Some even yelled obscenities. A large majority shouted they would be leaving town.

Helen made a left into her long driveway. A few feet ahead, metal trash cans rested on the side of the dirt road. Trash was all over the place.

"Those damn raccoons! I swear I'm going to take the shotgun and blast them all to hell," Helen said out loud. She looked left at the mess, thinking she had a lot of work to do.

When she felt a thump under her right front side of the vehicle, she panicked. Helen stopped suddenly and moved the column shifter to the letter" P" that stood for parking on her wagon. "What now?" she asked nervously. Helen wondered if she ran over a trash can or forgot to pick up Michael's yellow truck.

She exited the wagon and inspected the outside of the car. On the driver's side of the car, nothing. The front was intact. She began to walk to the passenger side and saw a single stream of blood slowly moving from the undercarriage.

"Oh no, what have I done? Not Zeus," she said, exasperated. "Please, please don't let it be Zeus."

She knelt to look under the vehicle, almost not wanting to, her fears realized: The beloved German shepherd was bleeding. It appeared he was seriously injured. Helen thought she needed to act and take it to the animal clinic. It was having a hard time breathing. She would ask Carmen to watch Michael for a few hours.

She dragged Zeus by the front legs pulling him from underneath the vehicle. The old dog was heavier than she expected. She used her legs' strength to pull it out.

Helen walked back to the car to get Michael. She opened the rear door, and Michael was no longer in his seat. His door was ajar.

"Can this get any worse?" Said Helen. Michael made it a game to get out of his car seat every time they arrived home, open the door, climb down, and play hide-and-seek with her around the wagon.

❊ ❊ ❊

Helen walked to the rear of the car. As she walked, she couldn't find Michael. When she cleared the bumper, she saw Michael standing next to Zeus.

"Doggy is hurt," Michael said while pointing at it. In shock, Helen stood by the side of the Jeep, not believing her ears.

"You spoke, Michael! Oh, my God! You beautiful thing! You spoke!" said Helen with teary eyes, forgetting Zeus' fate momentarily.

Michael crouched down and put his hands on the dog's face. "No, Michael!" Yelled Helen while hastily pointing her index finger." Do not DO NOT do that!"

Helen was about to walk toward Michael when what she observed stopped her in her tracks; Zeus started getting smaller. In a matter of seconds, it turned into the little puppy she remembered he once was ten years back.

Michael lifted his hands. The puppy rose full of life, playfully pushing Michael to the ground. He laughed as he fell. The dog's fur was bloody. Helen grabbed the puppy, her white sundress turning red across her chest.

Helen had a hard time keeping Zeus in her arms. The puppy wanted to escape and desperately play with Michael. "No, Zeus! Stop that!" yelled Helen, bewildered.

"Doggy better now," said Michael, sitting on the ground and pointing to Zeus. Helen was at a loss for words. Too much to process. She put Zeus down and carried Michael into the house.

The puppy followed, blood dripping on the wooden floor.

❋ ❋ ❋

Helen removed Michael's bloody clothes and put him in the tub. Nothing seemed to be wrong with him, not one scratch. Good. No blood came from him.

"Are you okay, Michael?" asked Helen.

"I'm okay," he replied while smiling and splashing the water.

Helen shook her head in disbelief. A few hours ago, he wouldn't talk, now he can carry on a conversation.

His unawareness of what occurred impressed her.

"What made you talk today? She asked him. Michael smiled.

Helen dried Michael with a towel that had wolves printed on it and dressed him.

"Go play," she told him.

"Okay."

Tiny droplets of blood intersected like mountain trails all over the house where the dog had been. Helen walked around them cautiously. She would have to clean it soon before it dried up. Zeus, or whatever that thing was, would have to be bathed too.

"What just happened? Was she going crazy?" She again experienced the same confusion and light-headedness as when she was at the cemetery.

She took the groceries that would go in the fridge and left the rest of the bags in the car. Helen needed time to figure it all out. She stole some dirt from a nearby flowerbed and sprinkled it over the blood underneath the Jeep. Helen returned inside to bathe the puppy.

While filling the tub again, she wondered how she would explain the sudden appearance of a new puppy. There was only one person she needed to explain it to, and that was Carmen.

"That won't be hard," she thought. She would say the old dog passed, and to minimize any trauma to Michael; she got a new puppy that looked almost identical.

Helen layered Zeus with soap. The blood on its fur immediately turned the foam on top of the water into a bright red color. Helen searched its body for cuts or apparent injuries but found none.

"What the hell happened to you out there, Zeus?" she asked while squeezing more soap on the sponge.

Too many mysterious events had occurred to pretend it was all normal. Helen thought she couldn't avoid it anymore. She recalled her mother's misty ghost at the cemetery, the bizarre way Michael had been born, and now this.

One explanation kept resurfacing; her mother,

Elizabeth, gave her an extraordinary boy as a gift from the beyond. She thanked her mother.

Helen looked at the ceiling aiming at the heavens." Thank you, mother. I knew you'd see things my way someday," she said, pressing both hands together upward.

Helen had a critical decision to make; what to do about Michael. His healing talent was something many would undoubtedly desire. If he were to be exposed, he would be taken away from her and be secluded in a lab for never-ending studies. He would be a freak, maybe an idol for some. She knew all about what scientists do to people when they become fixated on something. She read about a similar story," What was the guy's name? The one with an open stomach? Gosh, I can't remember this minute," thought Helen. In the article, a scientist conducted countless experiments with the man to determine how things worked during digestion.

"Oh yeah, I remember now, Alexis St. Martin," she recalled.

Helen dismissed the idea of locking him up in the house. That would eventually bring attention as people would wonder what happened to her kid. Also, there was the fact she could not make him a prisoner in that house as she had been.

She opened the faucet to rinse Zeus. The water came out at full force. Helen then had an instant realization. She felt stupid for not realizing it sooner: She had been tunnel-visioning on the blood and injuries and disregarded a vital aspect of the event; Michael not only healed Zeus, but he also regressed it back to its youth. Zeus was a puppy because Michael made it so.

Helen took Zeus out of the tub and dried him. The small dog started running around everywhere in an exciting way.

She went outside to gather the rest of the groceries. Helen noticed the trash was still on the road. She picked it up.

In the trunk, there was one of her leather gloves. The second was missing.

An idea occurred to her. Michael used his hands to do what he did to Zeus. Maybe, if his hands could not touch things with his bare skin, he would be safe. She would cover his hands with gloves.

Helen took the groceries inside and lowered the ladder to the attic. Up there, she opened the box labeled "Winter Clothes." She grabbed a pair of tiny gloves Michael had used last winter. Helen went to the kitchen and grabbed duct tape from one of the drawers.

She found him playing with his metal truck in the living room. She lowered her body to him." Listen, Michael; mommy is going to do something that may be uncomfortable. At least for a while. Just remember that mommy loves you, okay?"

Michael nodded slightly.

Helen put the gloves in Michael's hands. They were tight on him, but that was beneficial. He would have a more challenging time taking them off. Helen used duct tape to secure the gloves around his wrists. Michael looked at his hands, looked at her, and said, "No!"

"You have no choice," she told him coldly. Michael ran away screaming.

Helen started mopping the floor. It took her longer than expected. She didn't realize that water mixed with even a tiny amount of blood left the floor very sticky. She mopped three times. Helen put the bucket away and slumped exhausted onto the rocking chair. She felt physically and emotionally drained.

Zeus came toward her wagging its tail. She leaned over to pet it. Helen thought about the moment that Michael touched Zeus. She let out a big sigh. The dog had turned from old and injured to a perfectly healthy pup. Helen shook her head as to the incredibility of it.

VIII CASE CLOSED

The sounds of mockingbirds in the morning had become repetitive. Their loops and songs stopped appealing to Helen as anything endearing or unique. Their melodies somehow always served to be auditory reminders of the sins committed in that house she now wanted to forget. She glanced at the clock. The time was 7:17 AM.

She barely slept the night before--her thoughts filled with preoccupied images of Michael and his future.

Helen went to his room, her mom's old one, and Michael was still asleep. Helen tiptoed out of the room. One of the wooden floorboards made a creaky sound. She turned, but luckily, he was still asleep.

She went to the bathroom and stared at herself in the mirror. The bags under her eyes were a testament to her exhaustion.

"I will protect you until the end, Michael, "she vowed while grabbing the toothbrush. "I won't let those people do anything to you, "Helen affirmed, referring to anyone that was a threat.

She finished and remembered the turkey she had to cook. Helen postponed Thanksgiving for a day. No big deal delaying it. Michael wouldn't even realize what day was up. The previous day's heavy emotions had been too much to bear.

❊ ❊ ❊

The kitchen was small. The house was an Avondale Sears model house. A bungalow-style home without dazzling traits. Modest but comfortable for a small family. Her dad told her the previous owner worked at the paper mill. After the man's death, his children sold the house to settle an estate dispute.

Most of the appliances were still the original ones. Old and tired, they lost their maximum level of efficiency years ago. The stove showed the same olive-green shade, synonymous with old appliances like the ones displayed at The National Museum of American History in Washington, DC. That meant the oven would take a few hours longer to cook the turkey. Instead of four, most likely would take six.

Contacting Paul for any financial assistance was out of the question. Now more than ever, she had to make do with the small amount of insurance money she had remaining after paying for her mother's funeral.

Helen had been pondering about getting a job. She had been out of the workforce taking care of her mother for so long; it would be difficult getting back into the swing of things. Besides, Michael needed her.

Helen took the turkey out of the refrigerator and placed it on the counter. Zeus came through the porthole in the kitchen door with a dead bird in its mouth.

"That is a disgusting and unkind thing to do, Zeus!" said Helen while grabbing the bird and disposing of it. She had forgotten about the hole.

"Get out, Zeus!" Helen yelled. Zeus exited through the hole as expeditiously as he came in.

There was a knock on the front door. Helen stood behind the door. "Who is it?"

"La senora Carmen. Your neighbor."

Helen opened the door. Carmen had a broom in her hands. "I just wanted to tell you I cleaned up your driveway. There was some trash, and I don't want flies invading mi casa."

Carmen seemed older. Her hair was more silver than what Helen remembered. Maybe, she guessed, Carmen stopped dyeing it.

"Thank you," said Helen. Hoping the expression of gratitude would make her neighbor go away.

"A new dog is roaming around; a puppy," Carmen said.

"Yah," replied Helen.

"Nice. What happened to Zeus?" Carmen said while looking into the house above Helen's shoulders. "I haven't seen the old doggie out here like usual."

"He died yesterday, Carmen," said Helen, trying to sound like she just suffered a terrible loss.

"Died?" asked Carmen inquisitively." Of what?"

Before Helen could lie, Michael appeared behind her, making an engine noise while pushing his Tonka truck.

"There he is!" said Carmen while gently pushing Helen aside and entering the house. She grabbed Michael, pushed him up, and suspended him above her shoulders.

"What's going on with his hands?" asked Carmen, looking curiously at Michael's hands. "Why is he wearing gloves with duct tape?"

Helen started the monologue she rehearsed in her head several times already. She researched the dusty encyclopedia for a disease that could work until she could think of one more permanent.

"Yesterday was a terrible day, Carmen. Not only did Zeus pass away, but I also found out that Michael is suffering from hand-foot-and-mouth disease," she said while taking Michael. "It is highly contagious, and if I didn't do that, it would've been very irresponsible of me to expose you."

"Gracias. Rough day yesterday, eh?" said Carmen. "I bet you it has something to do with that damn lead water that's making people sick. I also noticed something that looked like blood on the driveway. Someone tried to cover it with dirt but didn't do a great job."

"On the driveway?" asked Helen, sounding surprised.

"Yeah, by the Jeep," replied Carmen.

"Oh that," replied Helen as if suddenly remembering. "I ran over one of those damn raccoons. I couldn't stand the sight of the blood."

"What a terrible day for sure," said Carmen.

"Yeah. Now, if you don't mind," said Helen while walking to the front door. "I have to go back to cooking. I postponed Thanksgiving a day. I'm sure you understand."

"Sure, muy bien," replied Carmen while putting Michael down.

"Thank you again for cleaning the mess," said Helen.

"De nada," replied Carmen while Helen closed the door behind her.

❋ ❋ ❋

One Year Later

With Elizabeth and Paul out of her life, Helen found time to take care of chores that had fallen to the wayside. The grass seemed to be growing like skyscrapers in her front yard. It was one of those tasks well overdue. The house needed a new makeup job, reflected clearly by the peeling white paint. The interior could use a good cleaning too.

She decided to tackle the yard first. Helen thought the old lawnmower would have a hard time getting the job done. She walked towards the shed. The lock was rusty, and she had forgotten where she had placed the key.

Helen went home and returned with a hammer. She hit the metal bracket held by rusty nails several times until it gave out. She took out the lawnmower and put gasoline in the tank. To her surprise, the machine started without a problem.

The lawnmower was noisy. It filled the air with smoke covering Helen as she pushed it. She decided to ignore it and finish mowing the lawn to the last patch. Once done, she stood to admire her work. She looked at the house one more time and decided to leave the roof and exterior paint for another day. She remembered she had to go to the market and obtain red roses, her favorites. It was Saturday, and the market would close in three more hours at 6:00 PM.

Helen was inside the shed returning the lawnmower when she heard a knock behind her. She turned, and Detective Aldie was standing at the shed's doorway.

"Detective?" asked Helen, surprised and confused.

"Hello, Ms. Baron. I couldn't find you in the house, and I heard a noise out here, so..." started the Detective.

Helen interrupted and did her best not to sound worried, "what brings you around these parts today, Mr. Aldie?" She said, dismissing his detective title.

"Sorry to disturb you, Miss Baron," said the Detective. She came out of the shed and removed her carpenter gloves. Detective Aldie extended his hand.

"I can't shake your hand; They are dirty from work," the Detective thought her hands appeared clean.

"That is not a problem," replied the Detective, his right hand retrieving.

"Is there anything I can do for you today, Mister Aldie?" Asked Helen, somewhat angry. "There is work to do."

"Being that tomorrow will be one year since your mother passed away, I want to check how you are holding up," said the Detective while bringing a folder he was holding behind him to the front.

Helen shut the door to the shed. "I'm well, Detective. Thank you for your concern," she stood and looked at him. "Excuse my rudeness, but I refuse to believe that is the real reason you came out here, to check on my well-being."

The Detective nodded reflectively, "after our first encounter; I considered telling you face to face what I think happened to your mom. It has been troubling me greatly."

Helen's heart raced. She started to sweat. She felt anxious, as if she were going to hyperventilate.

"Troubling! There is nothing wrong," exclaimed Helen, "I received the death certificate, and it shows my mother died of heart failure. You attempted to have an autopsy done despite my protests. I spoke to your uncle."

"I know," said Aldie, "He wanted me to apologize to you in person."

"Well, what you did, I don't think I can forgive. Now, if you excuse me, I have work to do," said Helen.

"Yes, Miss Baron," said Aldie, blocking her way.

Helen could feel his breathing on the left side of her face. "I won't apologize for doing my job, but I will apologize for not telling you my plans beforehand. But then I don't have to. Does any of that matter now?" Aldie said, tightening his lips.

"Exactly my sentiments, detective," said Helen. "Does any of it matter now?"

The detective put out a box of matches and a Montecristo cigar. He attempted to light it.

"I'd appreciate it if you didn't do that, Detective," said Helen.

"Okay, okay," he said while smiling and searching. "Where is Paul Thomas Jr.?"

Helen didn't respond. "Was he guessing?" she thought. "Is this conversation going anywhere, Detective?" she asked. "Because if the answer is no, and unless you have a warrant for my arrest in your hands, to be honest, I don't want to find you around my property ever again. No offense intended."

"No offense taken, Ma'am. I get it. I make you nervous. Or maybe it is not me but your conscience talking, Miss Baron. Consider that. Will you?"

"Detective," started Helen.

Aldie interrupted. "I promise you won't see me

around here ever again. You see, I am delighted to announce I'm due for retirement next month."

"Congratulations," said Helen without meaning it and feeling relieved.

Aldie crossed his arms, "the dilemma I have in my hands, Helen, is that my wife is talking to me about retiring now so we can move and live happily ever after in Florida. Then I tell her, some things will go unresolved here, and I'm not sure I could live with those."

"I don't quite understand," Helen uttered.

"I know that you killed your mother, Helen," said the Detective.

Helen's legs weakened. She started walking fast towards the front door of the house. Aldie followed and kept speaking behind her, "out of selfishness, hate, or compassion, either way, I don't care. There is no excuse for murder. After many years of detective work, I can tell you that I can smell a killer when I talk to one Helen, and I have to say, you are a killer: A brilliant one, nonetheless. My hats off to you. I should be the one saying congratulations; you fooled the system."

Helen walked to the front of the house and opened the front door. She placed herself behind it. John Aldie stood at the front porch.

"How dare you come here accusing me of something I didn't do," said Helen firmly. "Besides, sir, you have no proof."

"No proof Helen? Let's start by recalling how the doctor lied to me when he said you two weren't having an affair when it seems almost the whole town knows about you both. How your mother's eyes showed signs of choking, how your lover, the father of your child who happened to be the doctor, made the death pronouncement, I could go on and on."

"If you are so sure, why not arrest me, put an innocent woman in jail and embarrass yourself, Aldie? " said Helen in a condescending tone.

"Well, there is a simple answer to that; my Chief ordered me to leave your case alone. He said my ideas were crazy and unfounded. It all comes down to him not wanting a scandal in Edom. But I couldn't leave for Florida without telling you how I felt about the case," said Aldie.

"Now you have," Helen said, wanting to close the door, yet strangely, she wanted to hear more of his theories. She liked intelligent men. Even more, those that understood her devious ways.

"I keep asking myself how you stopped her from breathing: I found no bruises on her neck. You must've used something to asphyxiate her. A pillow, perhaps? Like the one that was on the floor next to her wheelchair?"

Helen swallowed hard, "as I told you before, detective," she said, "I don't want to see you around here ever again. If I do see you in these parts, I will contact your uncle directly and file a harassment complaint," Helen then started to close the door. "Enjoy your retirement."

"Thank you. I will, "replied the Detective, "and one more thing before I go, Helen..."

"What is it?" Helen was now peeking through a small gap in the door.

"Would you be so kind as to say hi to the doctor for me? After all, he must be pleased to have a boy with all the girls he has at home," said Aldie while turning away.

Helen closed the door and leaned against it. "How the hell did he get those things right?

Detective Aldie lit up the cigar and walked to his car.

"Absolutely no immaculate conception here. That woman is pure evil," thought the Detective.

With retirement knocking, pressure from the Chief to stop asking questions, and a wife who wanted to move desperately to Florida, he was forced to stop investigating. He had said his peace and felt better for it.

One thing will always haunt him; Helen would get away with murder.

IX THE GLOVER

10 Years Later

The night was surprisingly quiet. No dogs barking or cars driving by. Carmen had not visited like usual, and that was rare. Helen oddly enough missed her unsolicited opinions. She investigated outside the window into her neighbor's house. No lights.

Helen sat back on her favorite yellow-mustard-colored couch and knitted an almost finished quilt. She knitted a pattern of a lighthouse shining on a dangerous rocky shore. No doubt if the scene were real, the rocks would rip a ship apart if it came too close. The yellow color she used for the lighthouse light was brightly annoying. It made the quilt look cheap.

Michael entered the room holding pieces of dark red leather that matched the silhouette of his hands. Helen looked up through her reading glasses.

"Making new gloves?" she asked.

Michael didn't answer. He kept moving without stopping. He focused on the task at hand. Almost hypnotized. Helen waved to get Michael's attention, and he waved her off. He sat at the sewing machine and placed the leather under the fast-moving needle. Helen shook her head as if thinking "youth nowadays" and continued knitting.

The 1950's Singer sewing machine model 206 threaded efficiently under Michael's tutelage. Michael stitched the pieces of leather he traced using his hands. The appliance made a grinding sound synonymous with a lack of lubrication. Michael moved the gloves under the needle, pausing only to cut the excess leather and thread. He examined the gloves and smiled with satisfaction.

When Michael found the antique machine in the attic, he became excited. He could make things! The device was one of the early Singer models made solely out of metal. The apparatus was heavy. Michael had to lower it down with a rope. The thing felt like it weighed 300 pounds when it was only less than fifty. It had been an arduous job. He placed the Singer at the corner furthest away from her mother's couch.

The sewing stopped. Michael lifted his work to inspect the quality of the seams. Helen glanced at him and felt proud she "convinced" him to wear the gloves. Helen liked to use that term instead of "trickery."

Michael wore the gloves without much protest and even started making them on his own. She smiled while gazing at him. He turned his head and smiled in return.

His innocent blue eyes were piercing when staring, not the kind of stare that probes into hidden guilt, but the type that reveals trusted intentions.

Michael would inspect his work with the discipline of a skillful and experienced craftsman. A proficient glove tailor. He ordered the materials he needed via mail. The Montana hides and dye were cheap and easy to acquire.

Michael became an expert in the matter of gloves. He learned about incidental and intentional contact, abrasion protection, flexibility, dexterity, the propensity of the material to tear, and quality: all necessary information but dull stuff. Michael concluded that breathable leather gloves would suffice. As a precaution, he never shook hands or touched people on the shoulders, even though he wanted to do so.

"Tomorrow is a big day, right Michael?" asked Helen.

"The first day in a new school is never a big day but a bad day, mom," Michael replied. "You of all people should know that. It is that time of the year when I must explain to many in school why I wear gloves. Add to that the stress of the new nicknames I'll have to hear. It's a drag and got old a long time ago," he said while cutting the thread.

Michael lifted the gloves and inspected the stitching once more.

"Well, I won't call the school anymore to tell them you are sick," Helen said, staring at him through her bifocals, "Remember when you refused to attend the first week off Middle School because you were extremely worried?"

Helen tilted her head and knitted. "You can't live your life being concerned about people's opinion Michael."

Michael didn't appreciate her unwanted advice but told himself it wasn't worth starting an argument. Lately, it seemed they fought about everything.

Michael put the glove on. "A perfect fit," he said, raising his hand. He turned it side to side. He nodded with pride as he was proud of his work.

A yawn escaped him. "I have to go to bed. If not, I'll never wake up."

"Good night, hon," said Helen.

Michael stood and walked towards the bathroom. Helen kept knitting the pattern she liked to finish before the weekend. Helen looked at him, walking away. She wondered how long she would be able to keep Michael's power a secret to him and the rest of the world. She was worried. Michael was no longer the gullible and naive kid he once was. He was intelligent and opinionated. The best course of action was to continue to keep him under close supervision and sheltered.

*　*　*

"Get up, Michael!" yelled Helen. "You are going to be late for school!"

Michael heard her but stayed in bed staring at the ceiling. He procrastinated while counting the rainwater stains grouped like accidental constellations in the room's ceiling. It was annoying to think of the water that would seep through the ceiling with the next rainfall. A metal bucket stood guard to rescue the floor from being victimized by the falling water.

Michael was awake and had been so for a while. His worries about the first day of school had been an absolute deterrent to his rest. The sleep had been an intermittent one throughout the night, making the morning materialize slowly. The sun crept through the window announcing the imminent waking.

Today, not surprisingly, he hated the start of the day. Michael's anxiety about school had been bothersome. He placed the blanket above his head and wished he could hide under it and avoid the world till the end of time.

"Michael!"

He scanned for the bag he would need for school. The olive-green backpack sat on the chair as a soldier wearing a jungle uniform waiting for deployment on a secret mission.

Michael's room was small and customized to his liking. The red lava lamp that adorned his night table was one of his favorite possessions.

He liked the ever-constant flow of the hot compound that rose to the top. To observe the constant motion of the substance never got old. His mother bought it cheap at a flea market and gave it to him on his fifth birthday.

"Michael, what are you doing?"

Michael let out a sigh, threw the blanket aside, and turned off the lamp. "I'm up, Mom!"

He sat on the bed and stared at his hands that wore the yellow cotton gloves for sleeping. Michael worried what his new schoolmates would say about needing to wear gloves everlasting.

Michael had a few posters on his wall. One showed the model Kellie Durand in a bikini. In the other, his favorite comic book hero stood triumphantly, his eyes to the night sky and his hands on his waist, wearing black gloves.

Michael recalled how most superheroes constantly wore their gloves when performing hero deeds. It didn't matter what they were doing or how; the gloves always stayed on their hands. The heroes never cared if people thought they looked silly, strange, or creepy for wearing them.

"I will be powerful like you one day," Michael said while looking at the poster and slapping a fist against the other hand. He had become resolved that wearing gloves was a significant part of his life, and there was nothing he could do about it. Michael had just turned fifteen and wore an array of different types of gloves. He preferred to wear leather ones for their versatility.

Many strangers would often approach him and ask how long he had been wearing them. He would reply, always making it sound scripted, "I have been wearing gloves since I was little, and to be honest, I've never liked it."

Michael was as confused as everyone else about the need to wear gloves. Helen always avoided giving specifics. The truth was, Helen hadn't figured out what to tell him. She chose to explain repeatedly there was no other choice because otherwise, he would die.

"What you don't see will kill you, Michael," she would often point out. She had been successful in scaring him into complying with her lies.

"Michael! What's taking so long? Breakfast is ready!" she yelled.

"Coming, Mom!"

Michael ran to the bathroom and stood on the wooden stool. He removed the yellow "banana" gloves, as he named them, and placed them on the counter.

Michael took a pair of small-sized latex gloves, "the washers," out of the cardboard box. He brushed his teeth, inspecting their cleanliness periodically in the mirror.

Michael removed his pajamas and entered the shower. He washed carefully to prevent water from infiltrating the gloves. He exited, dried himself with a towel, removed "the washers," and put on the "bananas."

He walked to his room wrapped in a towel, dropping water on the wooden floor. He hydroplaned on the floor, ending at the dresser. Michael searched for his favorite t-shirt and found it without much effort. He smiled when he saw it: The black t-shirt with the face of his favorite superhero on the front. He also put on blue jeans and his favorite black sneakers.

He ran to the kitchen. The room smelled of eggs and bacon.

"Good morning, sunshine," said Helen, putting a plate full of eggs and bacon on the table. She glanced at his hands.

"Good morning, Mom," Michael said, sitting at the table.

Helen pointed to the gloves. "Now, Michael, I don't like when you wear your sleeping gloves to the table."

"Sorry, I'm anxious about school and forgot Mom," he lied. He remembered the rule but had chosen to disregard it.

"Mom? Can I ask you something" asked Michael with a patronizing tone and tilted head.

Helen knew his demeanor was the prelude he was about to ask something to her dislike.

"What is it?" she frowned.

"Where is my father?"

Michael played shyly with the spoon while avoiding eye contact. "I didn't want to bring this up, but as you are aware, I'm going back to school today. It made me think of the past first days at school. And I must confess to you; I can't take it. They make fun of me. They will call me names, which is nothing new. I know they will tease me about my dad, saying I'm a total idiot because he's alive and I think he's dead."

"Okay, Michael, that just came out of the blue," she said while facing the stove. "We have been through this a million times," exaggerated Helen turning around with a frying pan on hand.

"I've told you over and over that he's dead. Do not listen to those school kids. They are all jealous sonofabitches because you are smart and unique."

"But they keep telling me he is alive, that his parents know, that you lied to me and..."

"Stop it, Michael!" she said, "you stop it this minute!" she repeated while hitting the pan forcefully against the wooden counter. The aggressiveness of it startled Michael. He should've known better. Some things were just too dangerous to bring up; questions about his grandmother, for example, anything related to stopping wearing the gloves, the smoking habit she had recently developed, and his dad.

"Go! Get out of here," she barked.

Michael sat still, stunned at her reaction. "Leave now! I can't look at your face any longer!"

She gave him a death stare.

Michael was afraid to question the uncalled intensity of her outburst. He got up and grabbed his backpack, heading for the door.

* * *

Michael looked back at the house while running out. It was ugly, just like his mother's stubbornness. He was curious to know more about her inexplicable apprehension to disclose anything about his father.

He never believed even for a second his father was dead. And his mother hadn't proved the contrary. His mom's obscurity about that and so many other things puzzled him. All he wanted these years was his father's name to search for him. To confirm he was alive. His sense of identity depended on it.

Michael stopped at the bus stop. He cracked his knuckles while standing on the side of the road. He replaced his "banana" gloves with the brown leather ones he carried in his backpack. The gloves made a creaking sound while he stretched them. They were tight on his hands. He liked it that way. Those were his favorites because they made it easier to write in school. The pencil would slip with newer ones.

Michael also carried another cheaper pair made of vinyl in case any gloves went missing. In middle school, he had no other choice but to make an impromptu glove out of duct tape after losing one. He argued with his mom that he needed to carry more than one pair. She let him.

Michael thought he couldn't blame his mother for being strict when he failed to wear the gloves. He believed she had his best interest at heart by trying to save him from his rebellious self. She told him repeatedly that he could die an excruciating death.

She also emphasized countless times the need not to touch anything with a heartbeat, including animals and, most of all, humans. His mom would get so angry when she caught him without wearing them. Despite that, he felt justified in taking one of the gloves off while locked in his room. He had been removing them for years now. His hands needed a break. Nothing terrible occurred.

To his surprise, some people noticed him. The Edom Gazette reporter, Jeanette Wilson, attempted to feature him in a story. She told Helen she would name the article "The Edom Boy and his 100 Gloves during the unexpected call."

"Stupid title if you ask me," Helen told the reporter on their phone call. She had been furious that the reporter approached Michael at school without her consent. Helen sternly refused the interview, explaining Michael's life was hard enough already for the paper to make him their circus monkey. No way, no how. Helen's worry about Michael's exposure to the world was at the forefront.

Waiting for the school bus was not fun. Michael was alone with his thoughts. That was never good. His life would start reeling in his head, reliving bad moments like a silent movie. The downside was that no matter how the film started, it always ended the same way: the unresolved hardship of wearing gloves.

Michael lacked confidence. His gloves made him feel less of a person, isolated and unobtainable. He had been studious with never-failing excellent school grades. He thought he deserved to be allowed out of the house independently. Helen forbade it. "Only to school and back," she told him. His mother strictly disallowed any other outing: no field trips, no gathering with schoolmates, no social interaction, period. Helen's flexibility for him to attend school had been self-serving; she didn't want to home school.

A mockingbird sang in the distance and interrupted his thoughts. The song prevailed like a soprano in opera, muting the water moving in Pebble Creek. Michael tried to locate the thought-intruder to no avail. There was no question the bird was a mockingbird. Mockingbirds sound the same no matter their generation. As if their elders and parents before passed down their pains, songs, and tribulations.

X THE DATE

Of all the seasons, there was no doubt Michael disliked summer the most. In the winter, he could wear his gloves incognito without frequent inquiries that resulted in awkward explanations.

Michael concealed his bare hands at all costs to his schoolmates. The constant use of gloves had a definite impact on his hands. The lack of sun exposure made him develop a sickly gray paleness that was an absolute contrast from the rest of his body. They looked odd.

The only thing exciting about going to school was Claudia. Her green eyes and unique side smile were always gentle and never judgmental. She talked to him like a human being and not like he was a gloves-wearing freak. Safe to say, she was the only one in school that spoke to him that way; he trusted her.

He had steadily been developing feelings for her. Michael wasn't sure Claudia felt the same. He was so afraid to date anyone. His mother was too emotional. Unstable. He would be afraid even to mention it. He never knew what would throw her over the edge.

The faded yellow front of the school bus appeared on the hill as it had done for the last ten years. Not much changed since then; the bus bore the number 156, he was still wearing gloves, and they still heckled him daily for it.

The bus stopped abruptly, its hydraulic brakes loudly releasing air, the tire chains rattling under it. The door opened, and the driver greeted him. Michael climbed the stairs hoping to see Claudia sitting by herself once more. She was. Michael rushed and sat next to her.

"Still wearing the gloves?" Claudia inquired.

"Yep, still wearing them," Michael presented his covered hands, reciprocating with a smile. "How was your summer? How is it going at home?"

Claudia constantly argued with her parents. There never failed to be something they've done to make her unhappy.

"Summer was okay. We went to the beach. Nothing spectacular. My Dad and I argued about my allowance this morning," uttered Claudia while sounding upset. "Could you believe it? On the first day of school? He said I haven't done my chores and won't give me anything this week. There's some stuff I would love to get. I tell ya', at this rate, I will be able to buy something in the year 1999."

Michael laughed.

"Not funny!" she voiced, punching him gently on his right arm. She was a tomboy and one that enjoyed punching.

"My mom refused again to tell me who my father is," disclosed Michael.

"That is deep," reflected Claudia, thinking that Michael always managed to bring conversations back to him.

They both looked to the front of the bus in silence, pondering their frustrations. Half-opened, the window allowed the wind to insert itself, making a mess of Claudia's blonde hair. She tried to fix it. He liked it. It was the only time he would see her troubled. She always seemed to be so sure of everything.

"Would you like to meet for lunch?" Michael stared at her.

"I hope I can," worried Claudia without confirming. She made her long hair into a ponytail.

❀ ❀ ❀

Claudia walked toward her locker. Boys pretended not to look, but they were not successful. At all. She often noticed. "Why don't you take a Polaroid? It'll last longer," she'd often think, which some did without asking.

Her long blonde hair, intense green eyes, and voluptuous features attracted the most raging hormonal teens her age. Her face was beautiful, and it made her popular in school. Not that she cared about it too much. Many of the town girls her age envied her. For that reason, she was purposely quiet and kept mainly to herself. She developed a reputation of being arrogant even though she had not put any effort into being one.

Claudia opened the door to her locker. Someone behind her slammed it shut.

"So, Claudia," the intruder started to say.

"What do you want, Johnny?" she recognized the voice behind her.

She faced him.

"Please, Claudia, you know, that thing we talked about?".

"I'm not doing it," she replied.

"We need you. I need you."

"Get someone else."

"You are the only one that can do it."

"His Mom keeps a tight leash. He is not allowed to leave the house."

"How do you know?"

"I know him. Besides, my mom talks to his mom from time to time when she happens to meet her at the store," said Claudia.

"She told my mom she doesn't let him out without supervision because she is afraid he may get some weird disease or something through his hands. It may kill him."

"Well, good for us she lets him come to school."

"Right, good," agreed Claudia, only to get him to leave.

"I'm sure you can convince the "freak" to take a chance and come out tonight," winked Johnny. "Everyone knows how he feels about you."

"What do you mean?" she pretended to be surprised.

"You know what I'm saying?" Johnny showed a smirk.

The truth was Claudia had feelings for Michael too. She had not told the cynics she found his isolated persona mystifying. She admired the grace he displayed when he was the subject of mockery, which was often. For now, she would keep it only to herself.

She vowed not to hurt Michael since they started being friends. But she felt she needed the money. If she got the courage to go ahead and do what Johnny asked, she mastered a plan of her own for the night encounter. Before Johnny and his stupid friends performed their idiotic prank, she would tell Michael to run away and flee as fast as possible. She, of course, would keep the money. No matter how hard they yelled at her.

"Do we have a deal, Claudia?"

"I don't know," she said, almost convinced they did. "Find me at lunch. I'll tell you then."

"Done. I can pretty much tell that you are in; you are in, right?" Johnny said in a tone sounding like a used car salesperson. "You have no idea," he continued, "I waited all summer for this since I heard he was coming to this school."

"Whatever."

Johnny started to walk away but quickly returned.

"A quick question."

"Yeah?"

"I am curious. If you agree to do this, how are you going to get the freak out to the field when his mom won't let him out of the house?"

"You don't have to worry about that now, Johnny," she patted him on the shoulder, "let's see if I agree to it first."

❊ ❊ ❊

Michael walked hurriedly, looking down to the ground like he always did when he didn't want to be bothered. He was having a more challenging time than usual, avoiding obstacles like backpacks and the usual attempt by some to leg trip him. He felt like a bull running fast towards a Matador just because there was nowhere else to go but to the inevitable.

The collision came swiftly and forcefully. Michael's backpack flew off his hands, landing twenty feet away. Claudia's books rained on the floor, and she seemed upset. Michael felt awful and started to gather them, creating a pile. Claudia crouched down.

"Don't worry about it, Michael; I'm just not having a great day."

She changed her face to a smile. "How have you been? It's been a while."

"It has been a while!" joked Michael.

"Yeah, where have you been for the last couple of hours?" Claudia smiled. "I missed you," she told him with a simultaneous wink.

His heart raced. "I don't know. Someplace where no one knows what the math teacher is saying?"

They laughed.

"Lunch?" pleaded Michael.

"You are persistent. Yeah, Okay. I'll see you there."

❃ ❃ ❃

"What?" asked a confused Claudia.

"Like I told you," said Johnny while invading her table. "We need you to get him to the football field tonight. If you do this for me, there is going to be $100.00 for you in it."

Michael sat by himself at a not-too-distant table. He was having a slice of cheese pizza.

"So, what's your answer? Let's do this!"

Claudia thought of the watch she would buy with the money and other articles of clothing.

"Why me?"

"You are the only one Mr. Gloves trusts, and I also think he has the hots for you," Johnny hid behind Claudia so Michael wouldn't see him. He was afraid that Michael somehow could hear or make out his plan.

"Why tonight?" asked Claudia with some judgmental skepticism.

"Full moon, baby!"

"What does that have to do with anything?"

"You ask so many questions!" Johnny smiled half-heartedly. "Don't you get it? It'll be creepy, and not only that, but we will also be able to see his face when we do it."

"What are you planning? Are you going to hurt him?"

"No," Johnny shook his head. "Relax. We are not. We are just going to paint the weirdo's hands neon green."

"How?"

"That's where you come in. You'll lure the freak into the field tonight at eight and make him take the gloves off," Johnny savored the idea. "We'll take care of the rest."

"I don't know," said Claudia in a doubtful tone. "It won't be easy. Michael's mom won't let him outside of their home alone, only to school. I don't think I will be able to make him disobey her to meet me," she said while wondering how to make it happen.

"Well, you do what you need to do," said Johnny. "I'll be sitting at that table over there with my buddies," he pointed. "If you get him to agree, walk by our table, and nod. We will wait until the lunch hour is over," Johnny took a wad of cash out of his pocket and showed it to Claudia. "Just remember, one hundred bucks." Some of the other students turned to them upon seeing the money on the table. Johnny placed the stash back in his pocket.

"Two hundred," mumbled Claudia.

"What did you say?"

"Two hundred," she said this time very clearly, "I'll do it for two hundred dollars." Then staring straight at him, "Michael has been nothing but nice to me. I deserve more."

"Okay," said Johnny without arguing. "I can give you a hundred tonight and the other hundred later."

"Okay," agreed Claudia.

Johnny left her table. Claudia thought about the

two hundred bucks. The watch she wanted so desperately would now be within reach. Also, the jeans and the sneakers her parents had denied her.

"Even if he found out I had something to do with it, it wouldn't be a considerable loss," she thought. "He would most likely forgive me and feel satisfied he helped me get the money for the things I want. He is that kind of guy--a pleaser."

Throughout their childhood years, she had been guilty of using Michael's kindness to her advantage. She knowingly seduced him into finishing her homework, giving her answers to tests he had taken before her, and doing most of the work on her science class projects. If the past were an accurate predictor, he would do the same thing for her tonight.

Claudia grabbed her tray and moved to Michael's table. She sat next to him. Michael turned his body.

"I thought you weren't coming," he said with a skeptical look. He felt uncomfortable; Claudia was so close to him he could smell her perfume.

"What makes you say that?"

"I saw you talking to Johnny at that table over there. He is very popular."

"He asked me out on a date. I said no. I told him I like someone else," lied Claudia.

Michael remained quiet. Inquiring about who she liked and discovering it would be someone other than him would've been too painful.

"Michael?

"Yeah?"

"I want to ask you something."

"What?"

"Let's say you have a good friend that you liked for years," she started while appearing reflective, "and you finally got enough nerve to tell him? What would you do?"

"I would probably invite that friend somewhere quiet and have a conversation about it. That is what I would do," Michael told her what she thought she wanted to hear. He hoped she was referring to him.

"Somewhere quiet?"

"Yeah, like out by the river or something like that," he imagined.

"I like your idea. Not by the water, but how would you feel about coming out tonight and meeting me at the football field? It'll be quiet with no one there."

"Tonight?"

"Yep."

"The football field?"

"Yep."

"Me?"

"Of course, you silly goose," she said while punching him lightly on the shoulder.

"I don't know, Claudia. You know how my mom can be. I don't think I will be able to."

"Michael, I like guys who go for what they want. The type of guys that show me they are willing to do anything. Even if it is a little difficult? I'd like very much to have a conversation with you that's way overdue and maybe, do other things too?

"What time?" he asked, knowing well it didn't matter. Any time Claudia proposed would require the same effort. Once he got home, it was like being in prison. He would have to figure out a way to escape.

"I need you to be there at eight. Will you be there?"

"It is weird," said Michael while frowning.

"What's weird?" Claudia sounded defensive.

"I must admit I've never seen this side of you."

"Get used to it. I have been thinking about it for a while. It took me some time to build up the courage to ask. So, is it yes? Live a little. Will you?"

Michael bit his lower lip, "I'll do it."

"Promise?"

Michael nodded, knowing there was a high chance he wouldn't be able to show.

"Okay, see you there then," she said while standing up.

Claudia grabbed her tray and walked by Johnny's table on her way out. She looked at him and nodded slightly.

Johnny and the other three at the table exchanged high fives.

XI THE RENDEZVOUS

C laudia was not on the bus on the way home. Michael missed her. She most likely got a ride with someone who happened to drive their parents' car to school that day.

Michael thought of the meeting that night. He had difficulty mixing the excitement of meeting Claudia and the great fear of disobeying his mother. The dire consequences were unknown, but he had no doubt it would be nothing less than losing any little freedom he had left.

He wanted to meet Claudia later that night. For one, it would make him stop wondering once and for all if she had the same feelings. She implied and almost downright confessed her love for him. After years of wondering, the invitation to meet her had been the most significant indication. He chose to ignore the gut instinct that told him it was too good to be true. The chance to experience love came knocking, and he couldn't let the chance pass.

Along with romantic doubts, his so-called fragile immune system had been efficient brakes holding his feelings. He decided that would no longer be the case: He would tell Claudia he thought of her all hours of the day.

The school bus stopped. The driver looked directly at him through the rearview mirror, pressuring him to exit.

Michael exited.

In the house, Helen peeled potatoes with a large knife.

"Everything went okay at school?"

"Uneventful day," replied Michael. "Is it okay if I go into my room to work on my math homework right away?"

"Go ahead, she grabbed another potato.

Michael locked the door and removed his gloves, throwing them to the side. His wrinkly and ashen hands emitted an odor of a mix of leather and sweat.

The poster of supermodel Kellie Durand stared at him on the wall. She wore the infamous jean blue shorts that many criticized for being too revealing. He winked at her. Although she was much older than him, he often daydreamed of going on a date with her.

He would visualize both being on a side street in Paris, sitting at a small table in front of a solitary bakery early in the morning, laughing at each other's jokes like lovers deeply in love.

Michael saw his reflection in the mirror and thought his hair looked awful. He couldn't recall if it was four or five months since the last haircut. He could go and get a haircut and be back before his mother noticed. Risky, but the chance of a kiss from Claudia was worth it.

Michael went to his mother's bedroom and searched for money. He needed twelve for the haircut. He searched her drawers, and there was nothing but clothes.

He saw the crystal water bottle used to collect loose change on the floor, almost hidden in a corner. He grabbed it and flipped it over. The coins came out of the narrow bottle opening like a slow-falling waterfall. The flow of coins stopped, and Michael went to his knees to count. He picked the quarters and placed them in dollar piles. He was able to collect nine dollars and thirty-seven cents, including dimes and nickels. The rest were pennies. Michael thought they would be too heavy in his pocket.

"Damn!" he said aloud.

He shook his head, but he thought the hell with it. Michael picked the coins and put them in his pocket. The money made a huge bulge and weighed his pants down.

Michael never went out without Helen. She only allowed him to go to school after giving the teachers detailed instructions on supervising him closely.

Helen had threatened him with serious bodily injury if he left the house unsupervised. He was afraid of her. The look on her eyes was of a madwoman capable of anything. He knew she kept a shotgun secretly hidden somewhere in the house. He had seen Helen loading and unloading the weapon one night as he roamed when he wasn't supposed to. Once the lights went out, he was to stay put in his room.

The hair shop was not far away. Michael exited through the front door and started running. He held the pocket that contained the money to prevent it from making the loud clunking noise that incited unnecessary stares.

He turned right on Linway Street and saw the familiar wooden sign that looked faded with Lucy's almost invisible name. The sign swung with the wind making a rusty noise like signs do in the old western movies. He hoped the place wasn't crowded, although he didn't recall ever seeing anyone in there when his mother brought him in. He opened the door, and it slammed itself shut. A two-tone bell sounded advising his presence. The place was empty. Thank God. Lucy was sitting on a barber chair, reading a magazine. She put it down.

"Hello there, Michael," said Lucy.

"Hello," he greeted shyly.

Lucy looked behind him and outside.

"Where's your mother?" she said, appearing confused. "She's not with you today?"

Michael shook his head and looked down.

"Hey, it is no big deal, Michael," she put her hand on his arm. "I was just curious. She always comes with you. That's all."

Michael looked up, "can you please not tell her I came?"

The woman looked concerned. She held Michael by the hand and pulled him.

"Now, sit here and tell Ms. Lucy what's going on."

Michael sat on the chair. She turned him from behind, and he faced the mirror.

"I left the house alone. She doesn't know I am here."

"And why would you come here of all places?" She said, sounding concerned his mother may blame her for his absence. "Is everything alright?

"No, nothing is wrong," said Michael, "I just need a haircut."

"A haircut? Hmm," she said while grabbing the barber's cloth and waving it in the air to get any hair off it. "Something significant must be going on for you to come here without your mother knowing about it."

"I think I have a date."

"A girl, eh?" she asked while attaching the cloth around his neck. "I understand," she grinned.

Lucy grabbed a comb and scissors. "So, how long

have you been seeing this girl?"

Michael didn't know what to say.

"Is this your first date with her, Michael?" asked Lucy.

Michael put his head down.

"Don't be embarrassed; there's a first time for everything, okay?" She said, moving his face up to face the mirror.

Michael nodded. Lucy smiled.

"Before we start, I should tell you I don't have enough money to pay you in full," Michael said while shaking the pocket full of change.

"Don't even mention it; this one is on me," she said. "You just sit here, and I'll make you look like a million bucks."

"Thank you," replied Michael looking at her in the mirror.

"Not a problem," she said, measuring the length of his hair with her fingers. "So, what kind of haircut would you like?"

"Shorter and neater," he said, touching his head on the sides.

"Okay, will do then," she said, putting the scissors down and grabbing the trimmer off the counter. "Coming here by yourself was a big step, Michael. I am not advocating going against your mother's wishes, but a boy has to become a man sometime."

Michael looked at her in the mirror. He gave her a slight nod.

"I think a number four clipper for your hair will do the job," she said, picking up a plastic piece.

She clicked it in place, and the machine came to life, making the buzzing sound Michael enjoyed hearing. He liked getting haircuts. Even though Helen made it a point to instruct Lucy on the proper way to cut his hair, he enjoyed it. It was never the way he liked it.

"Maybe, it is better that your mother is not here with you," she said while moving the clipper to the back of his head. "That way, you can get your haircut the way you want it."

Lucy dropped the clipper and picked the metal scissors from a glass container full of a blue liquid. She also grabbed another black a smaller comb and proceeded to cut the top of his hair carefully. She stopped and looked at the hair at every step.

"Has to look nice, you know," she said, analyzing her work. "Does your mother know you are going on a date?"

"No," he said, "I don't think she would like it very much."

"Have you tried telling her?" she asked, the scissors stopping.

"I know she wouldn't like it for sure," he said, holding his hands up showing his gloves. Lucy looked at them in the mirror. "She wouldn't like it if I had friends."

"Oh, I get it," said Lucy. "She's afraid you may get sick or something?

"She thinks that I will do something stupid if I go out with other people. To me, it doesn't make sense. I mean, I go to school and all."

"Don't take offense to what I'm about to say, kiddo, but your mom is a little weird," blurted Lucy.

Michael took offense, "why do you say that?

"Well, we all here in Edom know she keeps you locked up in that house," she said, cutting another strand of hair. "That's not normal, and it is unnatural."

The conversation made Michael uncomfortable. Now, he just wanted the haircut to be over.

"I never felt like I could tell you this when your mom was around, but many times, I wanted to say that you look just like your father," Lucy added.

"My father?" asked Michael, very surprised. Another one of his mother's rules was never to make mention of his father. The man was dead. "You knew him?"

"I knew him?" she asked, "Why are you referring to him in the past? I know him, honey," said Lucy with an attitude.

"You know him?" asked Michael, now turning around to look at Lucy. "My father is alive?

Lucy realized that Michael had been lied to and that she had made a mistake. As always, she had said too much. It was one of those awful traits she always wanted to get rid of, but in her profession, it seemed like she never could. She stopped talking. She quickly combed Michael's hair and removed the cloth.

"Who is he?"

"I shouldn't, Michael. It is none of my business. You go on now."

Lucy pushed Michael outside and locked the door behind him.

Michael was upset. There was no use asking her mother about her dad once again. She would go on a rant like she always did. Or worse, he would risk escaping to see Claudia.

He ran home, and her mom's car was not on the driveway. "Where does she go?" he wondered.

He entered the house and searched for a hammer in the closet. He found a rusty one in a small wooden toolbox among a light green drill and a flathead screwdriver.

He went to his room and removed the nails, securing the window quicker than he anticipated. He rushed and dropped the hammer back in the toolbox. Michael ran to his room, fearing his mother would return and catch him in the act.

He lifted the window with his right hand, and with the left, he held the air conditioner unit in place. It was heavier than expected. He struggled and pushed the window down how it used to be, locking the unit back in place. Later, when the time came, the AC unit would drop to the ground. Risky, but there was no other way.

❖ ❖ ❖

"How's dinner?"

Michael wore a baseball hat so his mother

wouldn't notice the new haircut.

"Good," Michael daydreamed of Claudia while chewing on a meatball. Helen would cook spaghetti with meatballs when she didn't feel like making a more elaborate meal.

"What's wrong with you, and what's with the hat?

"What do you mean?" Michael's heart raced a hundred miles per minute.

"You seem, hmm, distracted, and you know I don't like you are wearing a hat to the dinner table, sweetie," she sat in front of him, putting her hand on his left glove.

"It's nothing. There is a math test coming up, and I felt like wearing a hat. I'm sorry." Michael looked down at his plate. "I'm going to go to my room now."

"Okay, I'll let it slide this time. I'll go check on you later."

"No, no, no, no need," he stuttered out of fear. "I'm exhausted and may go to bed early."

"Everything alright?"

"All is fine," he mumbled while walking his plate to the sink.

"Okay," she watched him walk away.

Michael entered his room and placed a chair

against the door.

The air conditioner unit dropped on the ground quietly. Michael let out a big sigh of relief, hoping his risky business would pay off with Claudia. He placed one leg out, then the next while looking back at the room's door.

The window was close to the ground--about four feet. Michael put one leg on top of that AC and moved the other over not to fall.

Michael started running out the driveway.

Being out at night, free on the street, was nothing short of exhilarating. The darkness of the surroundings did not feel terrifying. It was as if he were another nocturnal creature, natural in its dark habitat, moving about as if the sun was out.

The bleachers at the football field shone like distant silver waves while the moonlight showered them. Michael could see Claudia's tiny silhouette sitting at the top left of them. Her head turned from right to left and left to right as if she were anxious. Now walking, Michael hurried, stepping up his pace, worried she was afraid to be alone in the dark.

The night sky opened, uncovering the full moon. The lunar coronae that embraced it seemed strange and ominous. The passing cloud forced the shy moon to reveal its light from behind the veil allowing it to hide no later than a minute after,

* * *

"Hey guys, I think I can see him now. There he comes," Brian, the lookout appeared from underneath the bleachers. "It looks like he'll be here in less than ten."

Johnny spoke to Claudia from under the bleachers. She tried to warm her hands with her breath. Claudia was shaking, and the cold air was making her irritable. The temperature dropped to about forty-five degrees Fahrenheit. She had not dressed for the weather. She was glad Michael showed up. In a way, it was a sweet and sour triumph he agreed to come. Too sad she wanted the money so badly. Hopefully, she would be able to warn him before her friends did anything stupid.

Johnny spoke with the confidence of a quarterback in play, "Claudia, he'll be here soon. Just wait." she nodded. "Act cool and leave the rest to us. We'll be watching for the right moment."

"Not so fast, Johnny. Where's my money?" She bent down while turning her arm out and her palm upwards. She continued, "the deal was one hundred now and another hundred after I kissed him."

"There is no time for that now!" Johnny rushed.

"Fine. See you guys; I'm going home," Claudia rose from the bleachers.

Johnny reached into his pocket. A wad of money retained with a rubber band he obtained from school appeared in his hand.

"Hold on! Wait, Claudia! Here you go," he produced a small wad of money.

Claudia grabbed the money and started counting it. She held some of the bills to the sky, attempting to identify their denominations against the moonlight.

"Look, Claudia, stop doing that! He's about to find out we are here!"

"There are only seventy-three dollars here," said Claudia angrily. "Johnny! Don't tell me this is all you have! We had a deal!"

Johnny turned to Brian and the others, letting out a deep sigh, "that is all I managed to get. No one wanted to help out."

Claudia decided that the money she had on hand was better than no money at all. Besides, the allowance was not coming for weeks.

"Okay, Johnny, you win. I'll do it, but you still owe me!

Johnny displayed a grin synonymous with victory and resumed his quarterback demeanor, "Don't forget Claudia," the group gathered around him and listened, "once he takes the gloves off, you throw them behind you. That will be our signal. We'll take care of the rest."

"Right," replied Claudia, unexcitedly.

Johnny produced a white plastic bag from underneath the bleachers. It shook, causing the spray cans to collide, making the marble rattle. The group smiled, bonding while imagining Michael's hands wearing a neon green color. They ran to the other side of the bleachers about fifty feet away and hit behind and underneath them. Claudia walked the bleachers higher to the third row. She sat, rubbing her hands against each other, trying to warm up. She tried to find Michael in the distance, but the moon hid behind passing clouds once more, making it difficult to locate anything.

Michael slowed his pace when realizing he did not plan an exit in case things got uncomfortable. "Do I need one?" he questioned.

He would be thrilled to meet her. For his sake, he hoped this was not a sick joke. He questioned if he would be able to deal with it. It was flattering to think Claudia finally took notice of him. Michael resolved to act like a gentleman. His goal was to reassure her that he was not the freak they wrongly portrayed him in school.

He scanned the bleachers once more, searching for Claudia. "Why did she agree to meet me here? It is odd," he thought.

Michael stopped in the middle of the field. He recalled he had a small keychain light. He pulled it out of his pocket, the light coming to life. Michael tried to light the way, but the glow proved faint. He thought, "better than nothing."

He wondered about kissing Claudia. It made him anxious.

"Over here!" A feminine voice called, cracking the silence of the night.

"Yeah!"

He pointed the light toward the voice.

"I see the light, Michael. Keep walking straight," Claudia waved her arms in the air.

Michael approached the bleachers and stepped carefully on the stands. Claudia grabbed his hand and guided him towards her.

Michael saw that Claudia had a big smile. It was great being out. A lot better than he imagined.

Michael sat, and Claudia did the same next to him. She put her hands between her legs to keep them warm. There was an awkward silence.

"Must be nice to wear gloves, especially when it is this cold outside," She hoped he would offer his gloves to her.

He nodded without doing anything else.

"But hey, you made it!"

"Yep, I am here."

Michael sat closer to her when she trembled. "So? You said you wanted to have a conversation?

Claudia seemed uncomfortable. She felt awful for betraying him. She just wanted to earn her money and go home.

The air was cool, showing their breath as they spoke. Michael looked up. The moon showed a rainbowed ring around it.

Claudia questioned if she was doing the wrong thing.

XII MERCURY RETROGRADE

Claudia thought of the quickest way to get him to remove the gloves. She hadn't given it much thought. She thought she could probably seduce him.

"Have you ever kissed a girl?"

"No. Is that what you wanted to tell me?"

"Take your gloves off," she held his hands.

"Hold on a minute," he told her, removing his hands from hers. "This is weird, Claudia. I just got here. We've known each other for many years since we were little," Michael said while making a small height distance motion as to how tall they used to be with his right hand.

"We have been best friends for a big part of that time. Suddenly, you imply you like me at school and that we need to talk. I just got here, and without having a conversation, you are asking we kiss," he said, moving away slightly from her. "Trust me; I want to. But what's going on?"

"You are right, Michael. I owe you an apology. I am sorry. Pretty soon, we will be leaving for college, and I don't mean to speak for you, but I think we haven't been completely honest with each other."

Michael nodded in a confused manner while frowning.

"I regret I have not been more direct," she held his hands again.

"Are you saying you want us to date?"

"Yes," she said.

Michael half-smiled.

"Now, will you please stop being suspicious, take those ridiculous gloves off, and kiss me?" Her voice trembled.

"Are you cold?"

"You are kidding, right? My hands are freezing!"

"I have been so selfish," he started saying. "I'm sorry. You can wear my gloves. They are not gross or anything. I just made them last night."

"You made them?"

"Yep."

"Very impressive," Claudia said. "Well done."

"Thank you."

"But what about you? Are you going to be cold?" Claudia pointed at his hands, "I have never seen you without gloves in your hands."

She thought she shouldn't be asking those questions. The goal was to remove the gloves. And quickly.

"Oh, don't worry," he sounded like it was no big deal, "I always carry an extra pair in my back pocket just in case I lose the ones I'm wearing."

Michael recalled the beating his mom gave him upon losing them. Because of the bruises, Helen had not allowed him to go to school for two weeks. Helen called the principal to cover Michael's absence, lying they would be out of town on a family emergency.

"Yeah, I learned my lesson the hard way a long time ago. I lost them, and my mom got furious at me."

"Well, if it is not a problem, I'll wear them."

She thought about telling Michael what was about to take place. But she was afraid of his reaction.

"Of course, you can wear them," Michael said. "But you have to make me a promise."

"What is that?" Claudia moved her hands under her armpits to keep warm.

"You have to close your eyes," he said, "No one besides my mom has seen my hands, and they look kind of disgusting."

"But it is dark out here, Michael. I can barely see anything. There's nothing to worry about."

"I don't want you to be grossed out by me."

"Don't be silly!"

"Well, at least please turn your head while I change them," begged Michael.

"Okay."

Michael removed the leather gloves and put on the carpenter-type ones he had in his back pocket. He touched Claudia on the shoulder, "you can turn around now."

Claudia put on the leather gloves, "did you say you made these?

"I did."

"They are nice and comfortable," Claudia said. "You are very talented," she placed her right hand on his left, "I've never met anyone that could make their gloves before. That's kind of cool."

Compliments made Michael uncomfortable. He started talking about his mother just like he always did in conversation when he didn't know what else to say, "it came out of necessity. My Mom didn't want to spend money, so she made me learn."

"Well, regardless, it is amazing," said Claudia.

"Thank you," said Michael, "listen, I never told you this before, but I kind of like you."

Michael avoided her gaze.

"You do?"

"Yeah," she nodded. They stared at each other.

"Have you ever kissed a girl?"

"One time, yeah," he lied.

"Who?" Asked Claudia. Michael forgot she knew almost everyone he knew.

"A friend, you don't know her."

"Come on, Mickey, you don't have to be afraid. Tell me the truth."

Michael smiled. He forgot she used to call him by that name and how much he liked it when she did.

"Wow, I must say, I forgot about that nickname for a long time. You are the only one that ever called me by that name," he told her with a smile.

They both giggled.

"So?" Claudia said playfully.

"So what?"

"Are you going to kiss me, or do I have to send you an invitation?"

"I sort of have to go. My Mom, you know," he said.

"I don't think so, mister," she said. "Not before I get a goodbye kiss from you."

Michael moved his face towards her, unsure of what to do but willing to give it a try anyway.

She stopped him by pushing him gently on his chest, "with one condition," she said.

"A condition?" he asked, having no idea what she was about to say.

"That we both take our gloves off. A kiss is not a full kiss only if our lips touch," Claudia said. "I'd like you to touch me."

Michael had placed his hands under his lap and would rather keep them there. His mother had told him he could die if he removed the gloves and exposed the hands to the infectious world. But then, she had proven to be a liar. She had made him believe his father had died. Many at school had told him his father was alive. Maybe, he thought, that was the reason his mother kept him sheltered in the house.

But what if she had been lying about his hands

also?

"Okay," said Michael, "I'll take them off."

"You will?" The response surprised Claudia. She was sure Michael would say no or take a whole lot more work to get him to do it.

"I will," said Michael, removing the carpenter gloves off his hands.

Claudia also started to remove hers. She became worried, thinking about Johnny and his friends.

Michael placed the gloves on his lap. Claudia didn't take them and throw them as instructed by Johnny.

The clouds returned, and now a misty cold drizzle had started to fall.

"Listen, Michael; I should tell you something," started Claudia.

"Don't say anything," interrupted Michael, "I am just glad you are here." Then, without the slightest hesitation, "I love you, Claudia."

"That will make things easier," thought Claudia without saying a word.

Michael moved closer and kissed her. He raised his hands and held her face.

Claudia thought his lips felt good but that his hands smelled like old leather.

* * *

Brian hit Johnny on the shoulder, trying to be funny. The other guys laughed except Johnny.

"Hey man, that hurt!" said Johnny, rubbing it to alleviate the pain. "What the hell is wrong with you?"

"What do you think she's doing?" Brian looked in Claudia's direction, "She's taking a long time, and I'm bored."

"Yeah, what is she doing?" another one asked.

Brian responded, "I don't know, but if those gloves don't come out soon, in five minutes, I am going to go there and take them off the freak myself."

"Give her time. Be patient." Replied Johnny. "She'll let us know when she is ready."

Brian pushed Johnny, making him fall backward. "Hey guys, I think I have a pretty good idea of what's going on here."

"What?" the other two asked in unison.

Johnny looked at Brian defiantly. He was braver,

but Brian was more muscular.

"Is this whole thing to make fun of the "freak," or is it for you to spend more time with her?"

"What are you saying?" Johnny claimed ignorance. But Brian was right: He had a crush on Claudia and wanted to see her more. She had disagreed with his courtship requests many times.

"I am saying that we didn't need Claudia to do this," stated Brian, "we could've used her to lure him out here without having her in the middle of everything."

"Yeah, right," agreed the other two.

"We all know you've been trying to get with her," Brian said, coming out from behind the bleachers. "You know what? Screw this; I'm going."

Charlie saw he was losing control of the group and grabbed Brian by the shoulder, "That's not..."

A scream that seemed to rip the silent night apart stopped Brian from moving any further.

"What the hell was that?"

"I don't know Brian, but it came from where they are," added Johnny.

* * *

Claudia became smaller. A tingly sensation invaded her body. There was no precedence to what she was experiencing. Not one person in the whole world could describe it to her because she was the very first human being to go through the process.

Was Claudia shrinking, or were her clothes getting smaller? However impossible, the clothes explanation would've been a whole lot easier to explain. A few seconds earlier, the sleeves of her shirt had been by her mid-biceps, now almost to her wrists. Her trousers were falling to her hips. She felt terrified, unable to comprehend what was happening.

Michael took away his lips ending their kiss, his hands still on her face. When he opened his eyes, a little girl, probably no older than eight years old, was now in front of him.

Claudia looked at herself and then at Michael. He remained petrified in place.

"Oh God, did I do this?" he asked rhetorically.

Claudia let out the loudest scream Michael had ever heard.

"RUUUUUUN!" she pleaded to Michael.

* * *

Brian started running toward the direction of the scream, followed by the group. He retrieved a small flashlight out of his back pocket.

He turned it on while running and directed it towards the bleachers. He was much closer now. The flashlight revealed Michael standing over a small girl wearing Claudia's clothes.

Michael turned to look at the incoming group and wanted to run. His legs did not respond.

Johnny stopped and looked at Michael and Claudia. The girl was crying uncontrollably.

"Oh my God, freak, what did you do?" asked Johnny. "What did you do to Claudia?!"

Brian grabbed Claudia and held her in his arms. She put her arms around his neck and cried.

Michael stood still. The group turned to him, seeking an answer.

Michael was as confused as they were.

Without a flinch, Michael jumped the three rows of bleachers landing on the field. He dashed out of the park and into the street that swallowed him into its darkness. The group looked on. It would be the last time they saw him.

Michael's gloves sat on the bleachers.

XIII CLAUDIA

C laudia felt accosted. For the few minutes she had been back at the house, she described the fateful event at the football field to skeptical authorities surrounding her chair for what seemed the thousandth time.

With every request, their voices became louder and more impatient. It was undeniable they found it impossible to conceive a kid could somehow reverse time and turn another to a younger self in a matter of seconds.

In any other circumstance, they would've not believed a word she said and would take her fantastical storytelling as rants of a troubled youngster. Yet her parents and two younger siblings insisted; the petite preadolescent girl sitting there was their Claudia.

As if demanding proof of life from a hostage-taker, the police relentlessly asked Claudia intimate questions about her past.

No matter how hard they tried, her parents affirmed every single answer she gave them was factual. She even showed the officials the birthmark behind her right ear that resembled Italy.

Claudia went on to describe how her whole body felt while Michael touched her face, "like when you chew peppermint gum and drink a glass of cold water afterward."

"Send as many officers as possible to find that Michael kid," ordered the Police Sergeant to another standing next to him.

❊ ❊ ❊

The knock on the door was persistent. Helen cursed, having to get up from the chair to answer. Wearing her long black nightgown, she got the rope from the hook on the bathroom door and put it on.

"Hello?" Helen opened the door.

Carmen was standing there.

"What brings you here at this hour, Carmen?"

"Perdona, the inconvenience, Helen."

"Is there something wrong?"

"I was checking the windows in my house when I noticed your son's air conditioner on the ground.

I wanted to make sure you both knew."

There was silence. In Helen's head, theories about what was happening raced in circles like a ball on a casino roulette. She thought of Michael's homework and his need to go to his room right after dinner--all lies. He had planned to get out of the house.

Helen could not let Carmen become aware of her sudden anger and desperation.

"Thank you, Carmen." Helen shut the door.

Helen ran to Michael's room and tried to open the door; it resisted. The door had no lock. "Michael must've put something behind it," she thought.

Helen threw the robe on the floor and grabbed the outdated purple sundress from the closet. She threw it on, put on her black sandals, cream purse, and car keys. She went outside to Michael's room window. As Carmen described, the AC unit was on the ground, one of its corners embedded in the soft dirt. She peered inside the room and found no signs of life. A chair was leaning against the door, being held by the doorknob. She became enraged.

Helen ran to the wagon, rushing in reverse out of the driveway.

❊ ❊ ❊

Michael had never done anything like this, and it worried her greatly. He had always been secluded in the house and had always done as instructed. She hoped that when she got home, she would find him watching TV or sewing new gloves. "This incident is just a minor setback to our trust," she thought. "He went out to get some fresh air. Things can go back to the way they were: Quiet." She worried she was losing control and influence over Michael.

Helen slowed down, coming to a stop where some men gathered in a group. The biker bar behind them never closed, even as the hours of operation were "3 pm to 2 AM." Helen's brakes squealed as she stopped, the biker gang members turning to her.

She lowered the car window.

"How can I help you, Ma'am?" asked the biker with a long black beard and a big stomach. His leather vest, open and held together in the middle by chains instead of buttons.

"Did you happen to see a teenage kid run by here?" asked Helen.

The bearded biker shook his head. Another biker approached upon hearing the conversation.

"I have," he looked at the older biker.

"What did he look like?" asked Helen.

The biker turned to Helen. "Skinny, wearing a t-shirt and gloves, I usually do not pay attention. The gloves with a t-shirt made it weird for me; that is how I remember."

"Which way did he go?" Asked Helen.

"That way." The trajectory led to Michael's High School.

Helen took off without thanking them. The bikers shook their heads in disbelief.

Helen searched for about thirty minutes. She hadn't found anything in front of the school. Helen looked at her watch and decided it was best to head home in case Michael returned.

She was not far from home when Michael ran past her car on the sidewalk. Helen yelled his name out of the car window, but he kept running without even turning. She noticed his hands were naked and cursed at him under her breath. Helen pressed on the accelerator to catch up, but Michael disappeared to the left side of the house.

The wagon went fast into the driveway. The tires made an annoying screeching sound before coming to a halt. She walked steadily to where she had seen Michael, finding the hole that now replaced the air conditioner unit. She walked hastily to the front door and struggled to find the door key in the ring. Helen ran in.

"Michael, where are you? Michael, answer me!"

She searched the living room and kitchen in haste. The faucet in the bathroom sounded like it was delivering water at full force, and she moved towards it. Helen found Michael scrubbing his hands in the sink. He was sobbing, and a stream of tears ran down his face.

"Michael?" she called with a concerned tone.

Michael turned, showed her his hands. The hands were full of soap, and foamy water dripped on the floor.

"My hands are dirty, mom; they are filthy. I need to wash them." He turned again and scrubbed more with fixation.

"What happened, Michael?" she attempted to catch his eyes, "What did you do?"

Michael did not answer and placed his hands under the water faucet to rinse. Helen shut off the water and grabbed him by the shoulders forcing him to face her. Michael sobbed and faced down, avoiding her stare.

"Listen to me, Michael," said Helen. Then in a subtle tone, "I need you to get a hold of yourself and tell me exactly what happened tonight."

Michael cried and mumbled, "I touched her."

"Say again? I can't understand you."

"I was at the football field with Claudia. I touched her face. Something happened to her," Michael said among sobs and short breaths.

Helen remembered Zeus, their old dog. It had passed away a few years back of old age. She tried to block the image all these years when Rex turned into a puppy. The dog got a second chance. Now the memory resuscitated as undeniable evidence of Michael's power. The many years she built into trying to control Michael by lying to him and making him wear those gloves had been in vain. His power, used in a human, had done what she was fearful of all these years: It worked. It was a true calamity.

"Oh my God, oh my God," Helen covered her face in desperation.

She took a deep breath and ran her hands through her hair, trying to gather her thoughts. She then grabbed Michael by the shoulders and looked intensely at him.

"Answer me this, Michael. It is imperative: Did she look younger?

"What?"

"Don't make me repeat myself, Michael. When you touched her, did she get smaller? Did she look younger, Michael!? Yes or no!? Did she turn into a little girl!?" Helen's voice exasperated in crescendo with every question. She was yelling at the last one.

Michael frowned and answered, "Yeah, how did

you know? Have you been spyi...?"

Helen's hand came out of nowhere and landed on his face forcefully. His head went left to the point where his neck couldn't turn any further.

"You are such an idiot! You just ruined everything!" she yelled.

Michael's lower lip started to bleed. He looked in the mirror at the blood now dripping down his chin. Helen walked back and forth desperately and then stopped.

"We have to leave now!" Yelled Helen distressed.

"Leave?" To where?"

"Don't ask stupid questions and pack a few things quickly," She replied with exasperation. "You have less than five minutes."

Helen ran to her room and hurriedly pulled a small black suitcase off the top shelf in her closet. She threw it on the bed, doing the same with her dresser drawers.

Helen grabbed random clothes with no sense of planning and made a ball of them that she compressed into the suitcase. She zipped it, running to Michael's room to check on his progress.

She found Michael sitting on his bed staring at Charlie's Cartwright poster when she entered.

"What the hell are you doing? Where's your bag? She asked, frustrated.

"I'm not going with you," he stared at her. His demeanor had changed from upset to defiant.

"Excuse me?"

"I am not going anywhere until you tell me what's going on," he said. His hands were not wearing gloves; Helen couldn't help to focus on them. She had forgotten how pale they were, almost corpse-like.

"Michael, there's no time for that," pleaded Helen, "We gotta go," then stressing, "NOW."

"I told you already; I am not going."

"I don't have time for this," she said, walking out.

Helen ran to her room and went to the closet. She retrieved the rusty shotgun and loaded two slug shells into the chamber. The weapon made a loud metallic sound when she charged it.

She walked to Michael's room, shotgun facing forward. Helen pointed the barrel straight at his forehead.

"You wouldn't dare," challenged Michael.

Helen redirected the shotgun to the poster of Kellie Durand shooting a slug round. The shot hit it almost right in the center.

"Have you gone crazy?" Michael jumped and landed on the other side of the room.

Helen pointed the shotgun at him; "I will do anything to protect you from yourself, Michael. Even if it means putting a bullet in your head right this second," she said. "Just try me."

Helen pointed the gun at the closet, "Pack your clothes."

Michael walked to the small closet and retrieved two polo shirts off the coat hangers over Helen's watchful eye. Helen became irritated at Michael's seemingly blatant lack of concern, "You know what? Forget the damn clothes. Put on a pair of gloves and walk to the car."

"You just lost your mind," said Michael.

Michael did not comprehend what had he had done so wrong for his mother to be acting so irrational. There was no justifiable explanation.

The whole kissing thing had been Claudia's idea. The fact she had turned into another person was inexplicable and not his fault. Indeed, it wasn't his doing. No human being had that sort of power.

Michael exited the house, followed by Helen. She carried the shotgun on the side of her body, doing an abysmal job hiding it from sight. Helen noticed Carmen's silhouette peeking through the window curtains.

Helen and Michael were approaching the Jeep at the end of the driveway when Carmen came running.

"What are you doing, senora Helen?" asked Carmen, concerned. "I heard some kind of shot."

"This is none of your business Carmen. Go back into your house," Helen said while approaching the driver's side of the wagon.

"I can't," said Carmen, now noticing Helen's shotgun in her arms. "For Michael, no puedo."

Carmen grabbed Michael by the arm and pulled him out of the vehicle.

"Damn," Helen thought. "I don't need this."

The shotgun blast had been a reckless move. No doubt Carmen had called the Police. It was time to get on the road.

"Get in," Helen ordered Michael. "Get back in the car this instant," she finished firmly, now standing in front of Carmen and Michael.

Carmen moved her body in front of Michael, shielding him from Helen.

"Miss Helen, I'm sorry, but you are acting muy loca," said Carmen. "I can't let you take este muchacho in your mental condition."

Helen raised the shotgun.

"Carmen, I swear, if you don't move in five seconds, I will have no other choice but to,"

"Mom, no!" Michael said while stepping out from behind Carmen.

The shotgun blast was loud. The shot hit Carmen on the right shoulder, pushing her backward on the ground. The hole in her shoulder ejected blood instantly.

Michael looked at Helen and turned to Carmen, who was unconscious. He ran to Carmen and put both hands on her face for two seconds. Carmen's hair became less gray, just like it was two years back. Her wound closed, showing no injury. Carmen opened her eyes while taking a deep breath.

Michael let go.

"Get in the damn car," said Helen to Michael while standing above both.

The police sirens yelped in the distance.

Michael sat in the car and closed the car door. Helen started to drive away in reverse. Michael saw Carmen sitting upright while putting her hand on her forehead. She seemed okay. He searched for the rotating blue lights on top of the police cars that did not show.

Helen threw the now empty shotgun carelessly in the backseat. It bounced upwardly, landing raucously on the car floor. Helen turned left on the street, away from the sound of the sirens.

XIV THE
TRIANGLE

Claudia and her parents waited in one of the rooms in the emergency room at Edom Hospital.

Two doctors conferred behind closed doors about her case.

"I can't explain it," blurted doctor Wilson. "Her dental records show she is who she says she is."

"It is puzzling indeed," sighed doctor Diaz while comparing Claudia's dental X-rays when she was 16 and now.

Both doctors couldn't be so different from each other. Doctor Wilson was one of those doctors practicing for over 35 years and refused to retire. Most people called him "Grandpa doc" because of his age and gentle southern demeanor toward every patient and family. They even had a saying in town: "If you are going to receive bad news, better get them from Grandpa Doc." He was from a True North Carolinian. Born in Edom, he attended Duke University and returned to town after his internship.

In contrast, Doctor Diaz was young. She grew up with four siblings from Cuban parents who moved to Florida because of religious persecution. Their beginning as a family in the United States was humble. Her parents had encouraged their children to "go to school, obtain a job and be financially independent to have a better life than they did."

She attended the Miami school of medicine, and right after, like a cliché, with her eyes closed, she let fate guide her: she decided to hover over a map of the United States and where her finger landed, that's where she would go. The place was Edom, North Carolina.

"What should we tell the parents? They are hoping we can do something for her," stated Dr. Wilson.

"I understand their frustration. Trust me, I do. But this is beyond our comprehension and expertise. This case may fall under the CDC, hell, even NSA stuff. I have the slightest idea."

"Are you calling any of them?"

"Me? God No. They would make us the scapegoats, also probably Quarantine the hospital and throw everyone into a panic."

"Then what?"

"Well, let's deal with what's in front of us. We have a 16-year-old teenager who is now at her adrenarche stage. Some unknown change occurred to her cellular equilibrium that made her biological clock press rewind. The question smacking us right on the face is what made it happen. The kid who's on the run knows how it occurred or was the catalyst based on witnesses' accounts. He is the key. Without him, I'm afraid there is not much else we can find out at this point."

"So back to the parents. What are we going to tell them?

"We will tell them she's healthy, which is the truth. That we couldn't find anything physically wrong with her."

"We could tell them she will grow into a healthy adult. I'd think they would like it."

"Bad idea. What if her condition is permanent and she stays a child? We can't tell at this point."

"True. This is one of those cases that stays with you."

"No doubt."

"The main thing is to go out there and paint an optimistic outlook for the patient. I think it will comfort the parents. Let Rock County Hospital or whoever figures this case. There's too much at stake.

"Okay."

"So, are you ready to go talk to the family?

"Yeah."

* * *

The Police officer stood guard by Claudia and her family without saying a word.

"Does he have to be here? I feel like a criminal. Like I've done something unlawful," exclaimed Claudia pointing at the officer., knotting

"Sweetie, he's here to make sure you are safe. You are not a criminal. You are the victim here. We don't want him to come back and do something worse to you."

"He won't."

"You don't know that. How can you still defend him after what he did? Haven't you seen yourself?"

"Daniel," pleaded Claudia's mother, attempting to stop her husband from saying anything else hurtful.

"No, I won't be quiet. She has been saying all night that what happened to her is her fault. I'm tired of it. The kid knew what he was doing to her."

"Dad," protested Claudia. "I'm right here. Just because I'm little, you don't need to talk like I don't understand. The fact is I'm furious. I'm not only angry with him but also with myself. I lured him out for money. I agreed to do something I shouldn't. But you had to be there. He looked as surprised as I was. That's why I think he may not be responsible for this," Claudia pointed at her body.

The curtain to the small room slid open, and the two doctors appeared,

"Well?" asked Daniel angrily.

"We have great news," started Doctor Wilson.

"I'm getting my body back?" asked Claudia excitedly.

"Not quite," said Doctor Diaz.

"What the hell?"

"Hey! Watch your language, young lady!" reprimanded Daniel.

"It's okay. This is an extremely delicate situation," empathized Doctor Wilson. "The great news is that Claudia is very healthy. We can't find anything wrong with her."

"The hell with healthy,"

"Daniel!"

"Can you revert her to 16? That's the question. Don't tell me you have wasted our time tonight without coming back with a solution to this problem."

"We are very sorry. You will have to see a specialist at Rock Hospital. We do not have the capabilities to deal with this situation here. "

"A specialist? What specialist?"

"Maybe blood," replied Dr. Wilson, not knowing.

"Blood? What the hell are you saying?"

"Daniel, Jesus, don't make things worse. Calm down," said Mary Dwyer.

"Don't tell me to calm down. This is all your fault."

"My fault?"

"You told me on the way to the hospital you should've said no to the woman about not being fit to be a mother many years ago. You were wrong. That Helen woman shot someone last night and now is hiding her freak son from the law."

"Okay, everyone. We are aware this is not an easy situation. We are all on the same boat, trying to find an answer to what happened to Claudia. Doctor Wilson and I came out here with fewer answers than when we started, yet"

"What she's trying to say is," interjected Dr. Wilson.

"Yet we recommend you seek a team which could help you figure this thing out."

"What do you mean?" inquired Mary.

"There have been breakthroughs in cellular regeneration studies. One of them is at Freie University in Germany."

"Germany? And who do think is going to Germany? We can't afford it!"

"Dad, can you please stop?" pleaded Claudia. "This is not about you. This is about me. You are acting like you are the one that will have to live your life this way. You are not. I am the one in a 7-year-old body with a 16-year-old mind. I'll be the one dealing with the fact I may end up going back to elementary school and,"

"That won't happen," affirmed Daniel.

"Dad? What else am I going to do? Go back to high school and pretend nothing happened?"

"It's possible. You could be like one of those prodigy kids that make it to college before they are 12."

"No, dad. I want to be like a regular student. I want to go to parties, have fun and do stuff! I can't do those things looking like this. I can already see my new nickname, jailbait."

"Jesus, Mary, and Joseph Claudia!" said her mother.

"Okay, that's it. We are leaving," exclaimed Daniel. "This has been a complete waste of time."

"We are very sorry," apologized Doctor Wilson.

"You will be," threatened Daniel. "You will hear from our lawyers," he said while knowing he didn't even know of one.

* * *

Chief Carlson got off the phone at his office and looked at Sergeant Novak.

Behind the chief, the plaques and awards seemed repetitive. Most read: "For his number of years of service to the Edom Community."

"Well?" asked the sergeant.

Carlson shook his head. "Dr. Wilson couldn't figure out anything. He said the girl looked normal. There's nothing else he can do medically."

"That's not good," said the sergeant.

"I am not sure how much longer we can keep this quiet. I haven't even told the mayor. I reckon this thing is going to bite me in the ass. No doubt. The more people become aware of what happened to the girl, the more difficult it will be to keep it under wraps. Imagine if the press gets a sniff of what's going on. This may sound insensitive, but it is sort of a blessing the woman shot her neighbor. The press has been all over it."

"What about the other kids at the field? How long do you think their parents will buy the "you need to quarantine your kids until we figure out what's going on?"

"I'm not worried about those right now. The ideal solution would be to find that kid; we bring him back here, he does his abracadabra, gets her back to normal, and the chief goes home and is happy."

"I wish it were that simple," said the sergeant, resigned to the complexity of the case.

"Me too. Anything from the State Police?"

"No, not one peep. It is as if both vanished into thin air."

"Keep at it, will you?"

"I will, Chief."

"In the meantime, I'll contact my Fed guy in Raleigh and see what he has to say."

"One more thing Chief."

"Yeah?"

"You are not going to like this. But remember how the kid's birth certificate doesn't name the father?"

"Yeah?"

"Aldie called the office earlier and told me we should talk to Doctor Thomas."

"Okay, first of all, how does Aldie know what's going on up here, and second, why the doctor?"

"Some people still like him for some unknown reason Chief," said the sergeant pretending he wasn't the one who called Aldie. "He said the rumor goes that the doctor is the kid's father and that Thomas may have an idea where he is."

"Goddamn Aldie," said the chief. "He had the information this whole time and never disclosed it to me?"

"I'm not sure, chief. Aldie may still remember that woman's death, Elizabeth. He held a grudge for the longest time about how you handled that situation. I was a young officer then. I remember how he gave me a hard time for covering the body with a sheet at the crime scene."

"Well, now that we have the information, we must act on it. Go to the doctor's house and see what you can find out."

"Okay, chief."

"And Sergeant Novak,"

"Yeah?"

"Next time you feel like calling Aldie, don't. He's nothing but a pain in the ass. The last thing I need right now is his paranoid self, developing conspiracy theories from a distance. Leave him retired."

"Yes, chief."

* * *

The car drove slowly on a solitary road followed closely by a police cruiser.

"Please get back in the car Claudia," said Daniel driving alongside her.

"Leave me alone," said Claudia while walking furiously.

"I can't. You need to come home with us; you are still a child," said Daniel while smiling.

"Daniel, you are not helping the situation," said Mary.

"I'm not coming home. I don't want to go to school. I don't want to wear these stupid clothes and hate my life. I just want to get drunk and pass out."

"Claudia!" said a surprised Mary. She thought of one of his coworkers checking her household for violations after being reported for abusing minors by allowing her daughter to consume alcohol.

"I told you coming to the hospital was a bad idea, Daniel. The more people know, the worse it is going to get for our family. I wouldn't be surprised if a swarm of reporters is waiting at the house as we speak."

"It's hard, Mary. I have no idea what else to do. I hate for my little princess to be suffering this way without being able to do absolutely nothing for her."

"We can support her, Daniel. We can look at solutions together. If she is going to stay this way, we will have to deal with it straight on and make it comfortable for her."

"Yeah," said Daniel reflectively.

"I've been thinking,"

"Yeah?"

"Maybe it is time for me to retire. You and I had been talking about moving to the Triangle. Maybe that would be best for everyone. The whole family could have a fresh start."

"But your family, your job Mary; you love both," Daniel said, slowing down for Claudia to catch up.

"We can come and visit. And to be honest, I'm burnt out. The prospect of it sounds exciting."

Daniel nodded. "Okay, Mary"

"Stop the car!" Mary told Daniel.

Mary exited the vehicle and ran to Claudia, who was now on her knees, sobbing on her knees, covering her face with both hands.

Mary embraced Claudia, and Daniel approached.

"Let's start the search tomorrow," Daniel said.

�❋ ❋ ❋

"Can we please don't do this here, sergeant?"

The sergeant and Paul stood at the doctor's home office.

"What's going on, Paul?" asked Christine. "Why is this officer asking you about the woman who shot her neighbor?"

"Please let's step outside," said Paul pointing the officer to the front door while ignoring Christine.

"Paul?"

"I can't do this right now, Christine. I must speak to this officer in private."

Both men stepped outside to the circular driveway. Christine opened a curtain inside, attempting to make out the words. She only heard muffled sounds.

"I'm I in trouble, officer?"

"You are not, sir. And I am a sergeant, not an officer, please."

"Sorry."

"We are investigating what occurred at the Baron's household yesterday. As you may know, a woman was shot there."

Paul felt grateful he was not involved with Helen. "Yes, a colleague told me she's doing okay. She wasn't hurt. She just got blood on her from someone. I wonder whom. What does that have to do with me?"

"Well, we heard the kid Michael is your son."

"My son? Who's spreading those lies?"

"Listen, sir, I'm not here to judge nor to disrupt your life. I will tell you that if you don't cooperate, there may be other people coming back here that may not be as patient and understanding as I am."

"Like whom?"

"The feds, for example."

"But the woman wasn't injured. Why is this turning into a huge ordeal? Is there something you're not telling me?

"Please just answer the question, doctor. Is the kid your son or not?"

Paul looked back at the house, and Christine wasn't at the window. He turned to the sergeant and nodded.

"Okay, Good, thank you. So now that we have that out of the way, do you have any idea where they could be?"

"I haven't spoken to Helen in over ten years, sergeant."

"What about your son? Have you spoken to him?"

"No, not him either. I don't think he knows."

"He knows what?"

"That I'm his father. If he does, he never approached me about it, which I find hard to believe."

"So, nothing comes to mind?"

"Unfortunately, no."

"Okay then. You may want to stay in town. We may have more questions later."

"Sergeant,"

"Yes, sir?"

"Is there any way my wife won't find out about this?"

"I can't make any promises, doctor. I don't know how big this thing will turn out to be. And it seems the longer we'll go without finding them, the worse it'll get, so if you hear anything, please call me right away. Here's my card."

"Thank you, sergeant."

Sergeant Novak tipped his trooper-style straw hat and walked to his car.

Paul walked back to the house and found Christine standing at the doorway.

"You have a son?! And with that woman?"

XV THE BU

Helen placed the laundry in the rusted washer. She turned the knob to "normal," and the machine started. It made a metallic sound synonymous with struggle and lack of maintenance. Helen worried about how much longer she could rely on the appliance. She expected to be in that house at least for a few more months. She would not, in a million years, ask anyone for help. Contact with the outside world would remain minimal.

The small blue radio on the laundry room shelf played the top contemporary ballads. A DJ came soon after, speaking about love and happy relationships as the day was "Love Wednesday."

Paul's summer house in Malibu would make a good hiding place. At least for the moment. She wondered how long she would be able to stay without being discovered safely. Sooner or later, Paul or the police would find them if they waited too long.

Helen scribbled the address of the summerhouse house after Paul revealed it before passing out on one of his binge-drinking nights. She figured she might need it someday.

Helen and Michael were hardly speaking when they reached California. Their relationship had turned aggressive and full of contempt. Michael's loathing of his mother resulted from abuse, her lack of explanation about what occurred to Claudia and Zeus, and the shooting of Carmen. Helen blamed Michael for the critical predicament he put them in.

They arrived at the house mid-evening after a few days of cross-nation travel with almost no rest.

Helen couldn't find a key hidden anywhere. She entered the house by breaking the rear glass with a clay pot she found in the backyard.

Fortunately, the house next door to the right was for sale and unoccupied. The one located to the left was a few ways away.

"What are you doing?" Michael questioned his mother without fear. "Whose house is this?"

"I told you to stop asking questions. We are in this mess because of your rebellious soul."

Michael knew they were in trouble with the law. The news station spoke about them while they stopped for fuel at a gas station in Oklahoma. Helen pretended she didn't pay attention.

Luckily for them, the channel reception was bad and was giving an image here and there with poor audio. No one could make up their faces.

Michael thought all they had to do to better the picture was to send someone up to the roof and turn the antenna slightly to the left or the right. He had gone up to the top countless times.

The news anchor referred to them as "two people of interest," wanted for questioning about the shooting of a North Carolina woman and other suspicious circumstances. He was grateful to Carmen for coming to his defense. Michael witnessed the hole in her shoulder heal right in front of his eyes. He was glad she survived the shot. Michael knew the news referred to Claudia as the suspicious circumstances. He hoped she was well.

"I still can't believe you shot her," said Michael to Helen when entering the vehicle, sipping on an "I like Worms" Cherry Soda.

"Shut your trap," Helen turned on the ignition and sped away. The car left a cloud of dust.

Helen fled Edom without caring much about how they were going to survive. The twelve hundred dollars were growing thin.

Michael looked at the empty walls of his room and wondered once more what had taken place back home. The magnificent view of the ocean had lost its appeal obscured by the dark attic. He had been in that awful room for about three days now. Michael looked at the glove-less handcuffed hands.

Michael couldn't erase Claudia out of his mind. He kept reliving over and over the moment she became younger.

There had to be only one explanation: a scientific one. Michael hated science class. Yet, there were valuable lessons in some of the things he learned. One term kept coming to his mind: causality. Which simply put is the relationship between two things or events where one event caused another event, or several events, to happen. In other words, cause, and effect.

He touched Claudia, and she changed. Michael

had been the cause of Claudia's transformation, the effect. But how? He was just a simple teen-ager with no unique attributes.

He experienced a tingle as he touched both Clau-dia and Carmen. So what? That could not trans-late into the incredible.

He had so many questions. Claudia turned into the girl he remembered when he first met her. Was the effect temporary? To try to make ra-tional sense that Claudia changed to a past version of herself would not work in a million years. He couldn't consider any other prospect. If it wasn't, he had lost her forever. And that was worse than a breakup. At least, in those circum-stances, there was a glimpse of hope for recon-ciliation. Not so when your love interest is nine years younger, and you are still a teenager.

A vortex of emotions rotated inside him like winds throwing pleasant memories up in the air -None good. The forefront emotion was anxiety. The desperate need to know Claudia was okay and that she forgave him. A crater in his heart begged to be filled again with her smile and her personality. He wished he could turn back time.

Healing Carmen had been a knee-jerk reaction. He did not intend to do what he did purposely.

The event was still a mystery, nonetheless. But in these circumstances, the brain tries to explain it by believing it never happened. Surreal. Michael wished he could see her again. If only for one last time.

During the trip, Helen refused to talk about anything that occurred. She told him, "There is nothing to say."

Michael heard the clunking sound of the washing machine mixed with the muffled radio tunes sipping through the wall. He walked towards the door on the floor. He pulled but didn't budge.

Michael heard the steps coming up the ladder and jumped back into the small bed, pretending to be asleep. The door opened painfully upwards.

"Michael?" Helen went to bed and touched him on top of the covers. "I have to go out and get some things we need."

Michael turned his body while shaking his head, pretending he had just awoken from a state of drunken oblivion.

"What?"

"I'm going to the store. There's a list of chores

on the fridge I would like you to do before I get back," Helen said while removing the handcuffs, "put your gloves back on."

"Why are you letting me free now?"

"You've been an angel."

Michael looked at Helen without saying anything. He wondered if his mother had gone completely insane. She was different now, almost as something evil had overtaken her, leaving only the shell as a disguise. She was eerily lovely.

Helen turned and was ready to step down the ladder when Michael exclaimed, "Am I able to turn people younger?" He looked at her. "Is that why you made me wear gloves?"

A huge sigh emanated from Helen. Her tone remained friendly. "Now, I told you I don't want you to talk ever again about what happened to that girl. Our life back in Edom is no longer ours to live. I suggest you get comfortable right here and now, Michael."

Michael couldn't stop a tear from rolling down his face. His confusion overwhelmed him.

Helen stood at the door expressionless. Before climbing down, she turned to Michael, "please don't do anything stupid while I'm away. I do not want to do something we'll both regret. Please don't push me. I know it is fuzzy now and hard to comprehend what's happening. One day this will all make sense to you, Michael. Just know that I will do anything within my power to protect you. Anything."

His mother's words confused him more. Michael massaged his wrist.

Mary sky stretched. "Can you promise me that if I allow you to leave this room, you won't do anything that would cause me not to trust you?"

Michael nodded.

"I need to hear it, Michael."

"I will not do anything, mom," Michael replied.

Helen turned and climbed down the attic ladder.

The gravel on the driveway realigned under pressure making a crunchy sound. Michael went to the window and saw his mother driving away. She disappeared behind the dune. He wondered how long she would be gone. He scanned the neighborhood searching for signs of life but found none.

Michael looked at the sky and noticed it was absent of traveling clouds. The sun roamed freely, making the day a very bright one. He went to the window facing the ocean. An osprey flew in circles, searching Paradise Cove for fish.

The sound of the sea seemed louder for some reason. The sight of waves crashing against the rocks captivated him. He liked to watch them breaching, only to kamikaze themselves against the rocks that emerged from the water like accidents. It was the first time in his life to see it.

Michael climbed down and walked to the kitchen. The list Helen mentioned waited held by a magnet on the refrigerator door.

Michael,

1. Take the laundry out of the dryer and fold.

2. Sweep the floors.

3. Take out the trash to the bin on the side of the house.

4. Don't do anything stupid.

Love you,

Mom

Michael started folding the laundry. He stopped and listened to the ocean. He wondered how the water would feel if he touched it with his bare hands.

Would it be like the water in his shower? What would the taste be? Did he have the courage to go in the water? He thought of his mother's warnings and dismissed them as over protectiveness.

Michael opened the door. A salty breeze hit his face welcoming him outside as if he were the only guest at a fancy party; his arrival announced like an honored guest and well-received. Michael smiled and ran towards the beach.

The waves came and went, dancing in a pendulous swing that cleared the sand from any imperfections.

Michael walked, approaching the water nervously. He jumped when he almost stepped on a hermit crab that concealed itself under a small piece of driftwood. The crab moved sideways, defiantly keeping a watchful eye on the stranger. Michael walked towards it, and the shell moved backward, disappearing in a wave that carried it away. Michael laughed.

The water almost touched Michael's feet, and he stepped back scared.

"Germs are everywhere," Helen told him nearly every day, "and they will kill you, Michael. They are in the water, air, and everywhere around you. Be careful."

Michael wanted to touch the water. Regardless of what his mother had said about feeling things, it would probably be lots of fun. Fear had grown old and exhausting. He craved to be just like everyone else and not be afraid.

Michael stared at the ocean with a determined look. He removed both sneakers, placing them next to him.

He walked towards the waves. One small wave, without hesitation, received him gently.

Michael giggled. The freedom felt intoxicating. He dreamed of somewhere safe. Where would he go? The police were searching for them; his mother had gone insane and was keeping him captive.

The ocean massaged his foot repeatedly. Michael wished he could stay there forever. He inhaled the air and looked at the yellow gloves. He wondered what would happen if he took them off and touched the water. Michael stood and removed his left glove. He was about to put it in his back pocket when the yellow glove fell in the water. The glove floated and moved into the ocean, grabbed by a receding wave. He ran after it, jumping inside upcoming waves. He caught it, the ocean water now to his knees.

Michael was about to run out when a shriek ripped any ambiance. "Michael!" Then louder, "Michael!" His mother was running maniacally toward him. It took him a second to recognize her. She wore a red wig.

"What have you done, Michael?"

Michael grabbed the wet glove and slipped it back on his hand.

Helen approached Michael and shook him by the shoulders, "What do you think you are doing out here, Michael? Didn't you promise me you weren't going to do anything stupid?"

Michael stood longing for the freedom that lasted just a few minutes. The sensation had been worth every punishment that was to come.

He didn't understand the big deal. Lately, his mother has been more intense. He disliked her dramatics.

"I see that you again fail to realize the seriousness of the situation we are in," she said, pressing his arm forcefully, "this is it. Let's go inside; I'm going to clean you of your impurities."

Michael thought his mother's voice again sounded different. Evil-like. Like someone who pretends they have your best interest at heart, but their rage disguised as a gentle smile says differently.

Michael started to cry out of fear of the unknown. Helen ignored him and pushed him inside the house.

"Go back to the attic! I'll call you when I'm ready."

Michael climbed the ladder. He entered the room, tears running down his face.

The ocean waved like a new best friend. He imagined swimming in the waves like a dolphin, escaping everything. Especially his mother.

"Michael!" Put on your bathing gloves and come into the bathroom!"

Michael put on his clear gloves. The ones people use when dyeing their hair. He proceeded to the bathroom, and a strong smell of chemicals made him dizzy almost instantly.

"Get in the tub," Helen ordered.

Michael entered the tub wearing his clothes. It had barely any water in it. Helen got the metal bucket from the counter and placed it in the water in front of him. Michael coughed with the toxic gases.

"What did you put in here? Smells awful."

"Chlorine. Palms up."

Helen obtained the wired pad and scrubbed the hand harshly. She intentionally kept her hands away from his palms. She didn't want anything strange like what happened to Claudia or Zeus happening to her.

"You are hurting me!"

The plastic glove shredded off his hand, and the top layer of his skin started to succumb to the friction. Michael felt pain and retrieved his hand, freeing it from Helen's hold. She was careful now to touch his palm.

"Why are you doing this, mom?" asked Michael, "I didn't do anything wrong."

Helen grabbed the hand again without saying a word and scrubbed it harder under Michael's tears.

Once done with both hands, she took a towel and wiped the blood off. She grabbed a sheet of paper towel and gave it to Michael.

"Grab this and close your fist. It'll help with the bleeding. You are all good now. You are clean."

"Clean of what?" Michael sounded upset.

"Let's go back up."

They went upstairs, and Helen grabbed the hand-cuffs.

"Sit," she pointed to the bed.

She grabbed his right wrist and handcuffed it to the bed.

"I can't trust you. You will stay here until I figure out what I'm going to do with you."

"Please don't leave me here."

"You have given me no other choice."

"I hate you."

Helen paused. "This is for your own good. You'll thank me someday."

"You keep saying that. Nothing has been good, and no, I won't thank you."

XVI SIGALERT

Helen walked to another bodega looking for work. The woman behind the counter looked at Helen's wig, thinking it was too red.

"Do you have any experience?"

"No, I just need a job."

"Sorry, we are full right now."

The bodega had been the 5th store she visited today.

The few hundred dollars left were growing thin fast. Helen was grateful no one had come looking for them at the Malibu house. She thought she had no plan from here. The more she tried to come up with one, the more of a block she got.

Someone told her once, get the more manageable things done first, the harder ones later. She agreed, for now, that was the best course of action. She would keep looking for a job, worry about the rest later.

The local news had not mentioned any of the incidents in North Carolina. She wasn't sure how long that would last. Helen felt a sense of urgency, but usually, that requires immediate action. If she knew what to do, she would do it. The most important thing to do was to find a source of income.

One thing, she did know for sure. If Paul or his wife, for that matter, came opening the front door to their Malibu home with their key, she would run out the back. Probably follow Ventura Highway and drive north to Seattle. Maybe settle in Clarendon Island for a while.

If the police came, that would be a different story. They would probably have an officer waiting in the back for her to do just that; come out running.

She would have to explore how to get to the roof from Michael's attic room. That was the only chance of escaping without stopping the police from coming in by pretending she had taken Michael hostage.

On the other hand, she hadn't committed a crime. Had she? Michael had turned someone young, and she didn't know a law existed in the books against such a thing. Also, Carmen was not hurt. They would have to prove she shot her. In court, that would be her word against Carmen's.

The fact was, she was running for Michael. They would come up with some bogus charge, like discharging a firearm outside. Who knows, but they would take Michael, and he would end up somewhere probably not very pleasant. There would be nothing she could do about it if she were behind bars. And there you have it, that's why she was on the run.

She didn't like leaving Michael alone, but there was no other choice. He was too much of a liability. Michael didn't see the big picture. At any moment, he had thought of the immense relevance of his power. He was so naive to the evils of the world. If they came and found him there alone, he would have to fend for himself.

She was exhausted by what his disobedience had done to their lives. The promise she made him to "care for him no matter what" was conditional on good behavior. She did not know it came with conditions until it happened.

Helen stopped at the stoplight to wait for it to be safe to cross. She had not gotten used to Los Angeles, crossing the street whenever she felt like it. Jaywalking tickets were a thing here and crossing the road because she was impatient wasn't worth the hassle.

An eastern European guy wearing thick gold chains around his neck stood very close, invading her personal space. He had a three-day light brown beard and thick eyebrows.

"Excuse me, can you please not stand so close to me?"

"I'm sorry, Miss, my name is Dimitri," introduced himself, sounding Russian.

"And?"

"I've been watching you from a distance."

"That's creepy."

"No, it's not what you think."

"I help people."

"What sort of help?"

"I saw you go into that bodega and come right out. You came out with no bags and looked disappointed. My guess is that you applied for a job, but they had none. "How am I doing so far?"

"How did you know?"

"Going back to your earlier question on how I can help, you don't look like you are from around here."

"That is true."

The stoplight changed, and the cars stopped at

the red light. Helen stopped herself from crossing. She was intrigued.

"I give you money," Dimitri smiled, showing a
gold tooth.

"Give me money? That sounds fishy."

"You see, I help lots of women like you. A lot
come to LA to make it big, but they need that little push to get them over the hump. This town
will eat you alive if you are not careful.

"Okay, I think I've heard enough. I'm leaving
now."

Helen started crossing the street. Dimitri Followed.

"Five thousand. I give you five thousand."

"You keep saying I give you," Helen kept walking.

Both crossed the street, and Helen moved
through the crowd.

"Okay, lady, I'm sorry. My English is not that
great. You need money and me can give you a job.
I have a waitress job. I need a redhead. My clients
want it."

Helen stopped.

"You are going to give me five thousand dollars

for being a waitress?"

"Da."

"I don't speak Russian. Does that mean yes?"

"Yes, miss."

"Sounds like a scam to me."

"No scam."

"Just be nice to our clients. They will be happy to see a redhead like you."

Dimitri took a wad of money out of his pocket. "Here is $300.00."

Helen stood tempted but skeptical.

"Take it. I will see you at the Samogon Club tonight. 7 pm. Don't be late."

Helen took the money, and Dimitri disappeared into the

crowd.

Helen turned into a solitary alley. She counted the money, and the 300 was all there. She thought of going back to the house, getting back in the Jeep, and heading to Seattle.

A reality set in; she should be as happy as a

dead pig in the sunshine, yet she wasn't. Under Dimitri's kindness, there was darkness hard to ignore.

The tattoos in his hands seemed like unorthodox religious symbols done in jail by an amateur artist. And giving her the money without asking her a single thing about herself was in itself scary. Had he been following her for a while? Did he know where she lived?

Helen coughed. She wondered if she was getting a cold.

She would have to show up at the Samogon Club and hope it was a legitimate enterprise.

✻ ✻ ✻

Michael was hungry. The glass of water showed it was half full. He would have to ration it as his mother seemed to come up only in the mornings. The potato chips were gone several hours ago.

He had learned to hold using the restroom until his mother allowed him to. He wasn't sure he would be able to hold it today.

The issue of needing to pee was worse with being

hungry. The worst thing about hunger is that it consumes all your thoughts. There is barely any room for anything else. To think of Claudia would not help him forget. The images of her transformation came with confusion, guilt, and fear.

Michael thought of his room back home. Kellie came to mind with her everlasting smile that never faded. He would think of spending time with her. That always brought him joy. He needed hope to survive. The images would be their savior.

Paris was always the go-to. Not today. Today he would take her to a beach in Bora Bora. They would spend the morning at the beach. The afternoon at a water bungalow with no one bothering them.

She would ask him to share a hammock with him. They would look at the sunset together, eat pineapples and talk about the future.

In all the visions, he never wore gloves. Maybe it was his way of freeing himself from the burden. To take the risk of those things becoming the focal point of the whole encounter.

The sound of the Pacific Ocean waves landing on the beach outside the window made him smile.

* * *

Helen showed up early. The center console clock read it was only 6:25 PM. She couldn't find parking on the street and went behind to a narrow alley where a sign read, "No parking. Only deliveries."

She parked in the narrow alley and knocked on the rear door. A Latino short man dressed in a cooking staff uniform opened the door. "Yes?"

"I need to speak to Dimitri. He's expecting me."

"One moment." The door closed.

Helen heard a rattle and looked in the direction of it. A rat as big as a small rabbit was rummaging through a trash bag with a hole in it. Helen felt disgusted and relieved the rat wasn't coming her way.

The door opened, and the man motioned for her to follow. The kitchen was bustling with life. The smell of steak reminded her she had not had dinner. The man saw her staring at the food and offered her a dinner roll she accepted gracefully. It was warm and soft to chew.

Another door opened that led to a club lit with purple lights. There was a stage in the middle of the room with a pole in the middle.

"You are early!" Dimitri stood, widening his hands for a hug.

She let him for some odd reason. Helen guessed she needed the job, and the hug wouldn't hurt.

"I hope you don't expect me to," Helen pointed at the pole.

"Het, no," he laughed.

"I have a good job for you. Better than anything in here," he made a circle with his index finger.

"But I thought you said I was going to work as a waitress," frowned Helen.

"That's one of the jobs that you could do, yes, but I have a better one for you if you are interested."

"I knew this was too good to be true. I'm not that kind of woman."

"Oh, you think me talking about sexual meetings?" Dimitri made a hand motion of a finger going into a hole. Helen thought the guy had no class. "No offense, lady, but you are too old for our clients' taste."

"Okay," she said, offended even though she would've not accepted if offered.

"You drive a Jeep, right?" The cook told Dimitri about the car in the alley.

"How did you...?"

"Good, the job is simple. I give you medication; you deliver."

"What sort of medication?"

"Medication that cures people. Is there any other kind?"

"Well, where I come from, medication can mean different things, especially if it comes from an establishment such as this one. Let's put it this way; you don't look like our friendly neighborhood pharmacy."

"We help people. They can't afford medicine. We find it for them; we give it to them."

"You mean, sell it to them."

"Smart lady here," he smiled.

Dimitri had a black duffle bag next to him.

"First thing I'm going to give you is something that you may find scary. Don't freak out. It is for your protection."

"Protection?"

Dimitri unzipped the bag, dug in it, and pulled

out a small handgun."

"Whoa!"

"I told you not to freak out."

"I'm not freaking out. It took me by surprise. That's all."

"Why should I need a handgun?"

"The medicine you are carrying is very expensive, ryzhevolosyy. You will have to deliver it in some questionable neighborhoods. I would be very unhappy finding out you "lost" one of your deliveries to some punk in the street. You don't want to see Dimitri unhappy. Do you?"

Helen had not feared him until now. She did not know LA, and she would deliver to some who lived in "questionable neighborhoods" some medicine she didn't even know was legitimate.

Helen took the gun and put it in her back waist.

"That's why me like to see. Me knew you were right for the job."

"So, how is payment going to work?"

"You got two days of pay with the money I give you today."

Dimitri went to the duffle bag again. He pulled a small paper bag that rattled inside with bottles containing pills.

"Here is your first delivery, and here is the address. Take it there. Knock on the door slowly four times. No more, no less. An older woman will come to the door. You will tell her this word "Medikament." You will not go inside, and she will not invite you in. She will give you an envelope. You will not look inside. When you are done, go home, come back tomorrow. Me give you another delivery. Ponimayesh?"

Helen assumed the Russian word was the English version of "are we clear?" She nodded. She walked outside to her car and wondered what the hell she had just gotten herself into.

* * *

Helen looked at the address: The awful handwriting read 1443 West E Street, Wilmington, LA. She grabbed the map atlas.

The house address was across town to the south.

It would take her at least 40 minutes to get there. By the time she delivered the medication and drove back to Malibu's house, the time would be about 11 to 11:30 PM. Michael would be unhappy.

Helen drove, turning left onto Arlington Avenue.

She would end up taking the 110 south, down Wilmington.

She looked at the different neighborhoods while driving by; Arlington Heights, West Adams, Athens, South Park, Pico. The contrast of the concrete jungle from the trees-filled town of Edom couldn't be more obvious. LA had too many people. Too many cars. And something as menial as meeting a foreigner was unheard of in Edom. She had never met a Russian person in her life.

Helen's stomach growled loudly. The bread roll she had eaten earlier was gone from her system. She wanted to stop and get some food but delivering the package was a priority. She would look for a place afterward.

Exit 3B came quicker than she expected. She took a right from Figueroa Place and the humble small yellow house showing large 1443 numbers under a front porch light.

The house was a corner house. Helen parked in the driveway behind an old car. An older woman in the house opened the curtain, quickly closing it.

Helen knocked on the front door four times. The

house was dark. The older woman, probably in her 70's opened the door, the chain door holding it from spreading more. The woman was short, wearing a nightgown the type that older women wear.

"Hello? Medication?" Helen greeted.

The woman stared at Helen. A thick yellow envelope appeared through the aperture, and Helen took it. The empty hand then waited for Helen. She put the bag into the woman's hand, who made it disappear behind the door. The door slammed closed.

"Okay. That was weird," said Helen.

Helen started driving, taking the 110 back north.

* * *

Michael woke up with the sound of the door opening downstairs. He heard the attic ladder lowering, and the floor door sprung open. Helen walked to the light switch and flipped it up.

Helen saw the puddle of urine on the floor.

"For God's sake! Couldn't you hold it till I got home? Now I have to clean this mess."

"You have been gone since the morning. I think you should show some compassion and admit this is your fault," Michael retorted.

"Here's a burrito," said Helen.

Michael wanted to argue more and maybe punch her in the face. No one should put a human being through this.

Helen took the handcuff key out of her pocket. She put the key in the small hole, careful not to touch Michael's glove.

"What's a burrito?"

"I can't believe you are that sheltered," Helen shook her head. "Regardless, you'll like it."

Helen watched Michael eat.

"I got a job today. It pays very well. I think we will be able to leave here very soon."

"Again? To where? I don't want to spend the rest of my life running and handcuffed to a bed. I'm still not even sure what happened back home.

You won't say anything."

"Eat," ordered Helen. "Once you eat, I want you to take a shower while I clean this mess."

Helen coughed. A drop of blood stained the palm of her hand.

"What's that, blood?"

"I don't know, Michael. It looks like it. It just started happening this morning."

Michael took another bite of the burrito.

"How much longer will I have to be here?"

"I hope to do the new job for a few more days. Then we'll see."

"I can't live like this, Helen."

"Mom, not Helen."

"If you act like a mom, then I'll call you one. Otherwise, it is going to be Helen.

XVII GOODBYE MOTHER

Three Days Later

Helen appeared at the Club bright and early. It was 5:30 AM. She was getting paid by the day and had several deliveries to make all over town.

She entered the Club, and Dimitri was cleaning the bar.

"Don't you ever go home?" joked Helen.

"Beregi plat'ye snovu, a chest' smolodu, ryzhevolosyy. I'm not a young man anymore. I have no time to waste."

"I told you I don't speak Russian. What does that mean?"

"For you Amerikan, it means, those who would be young when they are old must be old when they are young."

"Okay," said Helen, confused. She coughed on a white napkin. The blood made It bright red.

"Please sit," he pointed at a table.

Helen frowned and sat.

"Me like you. You do good job. I have bad news."
"What? What did I do?"

"You are sick. I can't have you deliver medikament to customers when you are coughing blood. It makes them feel, you know, uncomfortable."

Helen hoped he wouldn't notice. She could hardly control her cough any longer. "But this is temporary. I will get better," Helen knew that wasn't true. The free clinic had told her she needed Tuberculosis treatment asap. They had given her a mask to wear, but she didn't want Dimitri to see her wearing it.

"It's good. I have other lady starting today. You come back later when you better."

"Don't you have medicine? Can't you give me something to make it better?"

"Our medikament is platsebo. How do me say? Like candy?"

Helen left quietly. She sat in her car confused, upset, and hopeless. She honestly had no idea about the medication. "I'm so naive," she thought. She pondered about the future. There was none. Not without curing the illness first. She had been afraid to ask Michael for help. She did not want to end up like Claudia: a small child. The thought terrified her.

Unfortunately, there were only two options left: Have Michael do his thing on her or die.

* * *

Michael awoke with the cricket's stridulation. Unlike a rooster's crow, the bug's chirping exerted annoyed urgency to get up and do nothing. He opened his eyes. With no clock and the sun barely showing, he guessed the time to be 6 am.

The simple three-step process of waking up went in the following order: opening of eyes, realizing he remained a prisoner, and wondering how much longer.

There was absolutely nothing to do in that godforsaken room but to stare at the ocean all day. The occasional rain served as a welcomed distraction. The sometimes-muffled sounds of the airborne songs vibrating through the wall helped keep him stay sane.

He had no idea how long he remained handcuffed to the bed after the beach incident. His mother came to check on him every morning, gave him food, and always wore the stupid red wig. Her face was sunken. For the last few days, she was disheveled and tired. Michael guessed the stress of the hiding became too much for her.

He examined the left wrist. The skin had almost healed, but the injury remained painful. He had pulled on the handcuffs to try to set himself free. In the battle against metal and skin, no doubt metal was always the overpowering bully.

Michael had not seen the outside of the room in weeks. He lost count of the days.

Michael started wishing his mother would go away. But not before he went free. It could be easy; they would agree to go their separate ways without making a big fuss.

Helen became his captor. The bond between mother and son no longer existed. In Michael's eyes, keeping him against his will was the worst thing of them all, a significant black checkmark in the long list of things she had done against him in the last few months.

The sun entered the room, heating his leg. Michael let out a big sigh. By mid-morning, the temperature in the attic would become hot.

The ladder lowered with the usual rattling of the keys soon after. Helen sounded like she coughed up a lung while climbing.

Helen entered the room with a bowl of oatmeal and placed it next to him. She coughed into her hand, blood landing on her palm.

Michael frowned. Helen wiped her hand with a hand towel she had in her jeans' back pocket.

"I'm sick. I did what I needed to do to keep the income coming in. To be able to feed you. To be a good mother to you."

Michael's confusion-exhaustion became a primary emotion. It made him muted.

"I am in desperate need of your help Michael."

Helen had been diagnosed in the free medical clinic in downtown Los Angeles with tuberculosis. She was told it was serious. She started treatment and stopped after the first visit. She had to flee when recognized by one of the nurses. "Wait a minute, aren't you that lady on the news with the teenage kid? The one running from the cops. Oh, my god!"

Helen gave her the standard cliché answer most criminals say in movies when identified: "That's not me. I have no idea what you are talking about." She then left in a hurry.

Helen was sure that day would come: That episode in her life where the infamous fugitive is recognized by another who paid attention. As much as she prepared for the moment, it upset her. That encounter thwarted any other tuberculosis treatments. Helen hoped her illness would go away with only the first treatment. It did not.

Michael's hunger dominated him above all else. He grabbed the bowl and gulped the oatmeal.

"I must explain some things, Michael, you should be aware of," Helen said while removing the cuff. "I will start by telling you that I think I'm dying," she said.

Michael showed no empathy. He took her statement as another attempt to try to dismiss the pain she put him through. To undermine the wrong and elevate herself into the victim role. He learned to hate her for what she had done to him.

"Please don't be upset about what I'm about to tell you."

Michael couldn't keep the oath he made to himself of never speaking to her, ever again.

"What?"

"Your father is not dead."

"What?!"

"He is alive. He is Doctor Paul Thomas. I am sure you know of him."

"My dad lives in our town? Why did you lie to me and make me believe my father died? Lucy was right."

"Lucy, she told you? When did this happen?"

"I went to get a haircut alone. She told me my dad wasn't dead."

"That bitch!"

"It is not her fault, and it is not about her. Tell me the truth."

"She shouldn't have."

"Never mind that."

It is complicated, Michael. I need to explain. There is one primary reason that justifies why I raised you the way I did," she said while covering her mouth with her right hand. She coughed. The fatigue, combined with the blood coming out of her lungs, made her conclude she probably had little time left.

"You see," Helen raised her voice, trying to gather

strength. "When you were four years old, I ran over Zeus in our driveway. He bled and,"

"Zeus, our dog? But how is it that he ran around as if nothing happened? Did he have surgery?"

"No. Zeus didn't have surgery. You did it, Michael. You saved him."

"I did what? You are crazy. Didn't you say I was four years old?"

"Listen, you did something extraordinary that day. I hoped that the miracle I witnessed had been a one-time thing, but you proved me wrong when you touched that girl, and then Carmen."

"I don't understand."

"I ran over Zeus accidentally. He was badly hurt. I remember it like it was yesterday. It was Thanksgiving; we were coming back home from the store," Helen smiled. "I wanted to make Thanksgiving special for the both of us. After I went to see what happened, I saw Zeus almost dead," Helen looked down and pointed at the floor, "He was bleeding. A lot. I thought it was over for him. Almost as if the weight of the vehicle squeezed his insides right out of its mouth. I didn't want you to experience that. I went to look for you back in the Jeep, but you were not inside. It is all clear to me now. Subconsciously, you've always known you had this power."

Michael thought his mother had gone officially mad.

"You touched the dog Michael with both of your small hands. And right in front of my eyes, it turned into a puppy. All cured, healed, and healthy."

"I'm sorry. This is too much. I don't believe anything you are telling me."

"That is why I made you wear the gloves. So, people wouldn't find out what you could do. You have a gift Michael, and I'm in urgent need."

"But my father..." started Michael.

"Did you listen to what I told you?"

"Yeah, yeah, sure, I have a "great power," blah, blah, blah," Michael said while drawing quotation marks in the air.

"Why are you so cynical?"

"Hmm, let's go down the list. You act crazy, made me a prisoner in this attic, and handcuffed me to this bed for months. You lied about my father and made me wear these gloves, making me believe I was allergic to the world. Should I continue?"

"Okay, genius, if I'm so crazy, how do you explain what you did to Claudia? To Carmen? You told me in your own words that you..."

"It was dark. Maybe I did nothing to Claudia. She is fine back home for all we know, and perhaps, just perhaps, Carmen is dead. You did shoot her, remember?

Helen wanted to continue, to prove him wrong. She paused when needing to cough. The towel showed a circular red blood spot.

"I know you have suffered. I'm sorry. But just like you, I was a prisoner once too. I cared for your grandmother for years: I fed her, bathed her, cleaned her, and for what? I wasted my youth there. Finally, I couldn't take it anymore. She had to go."

"Jesus, you killed her?"

Helen shook her head and stared at the floor with a blank stare. She then got on the floor and started knee walking toward Michael. "Touch my face with your bare hands, Michael. Please do it. Please," she begged with a tearful tone. "See for yourself once more what you are capable of doing. Cure me. That is the least I deserve."

Michael was in shock, processing her confessions.

"I won't touch you."

"If you don't, you will never leave this place alive. I promise you. I'll leave your body to rot in here. What do I care? I'll be dead soon anyway."

"You wouldn't."

"I have a small gun in my back waist. I will use it if necessary."

Michael felt there was no use in arguing. His mother proved faithful to her malignant promises. He had no other choice but to do what she asked, to touch her. There was no way out of that room otherwise. She would do anything in her power to stop him if he tried to escape.

Michael hated her now. The love for her was a dysfunctional brainwash conditioned to believe there was no future without her. Helen always reminded him that wearing the gloves did not mean he was a freak. She told him he was normal when she knew well, he was different. He lost faith in the world.

He despised her more than ever for what she stood for, dishonesty, betrayal, and malice. Michael wished she disappeared out of his life.

Michael removed his gloves. He thought if his hands' power worked, she would leave him alone, happy, and let him free. She smiled while moving closer. He sat at the edge of the bed, opening his hands in a welcoming manner. Helen knelt slowly, closing her eyes and inserting her face in the space between the hands. Michael compressed them against her cheeks.

"I hate you," he cried, feeling the tingle on the palm of his hands.

"What did you say?"

Helen started to look old. Much older. The wrinkles appeared instantaneously like hundreds of dried rivers in the desert seen from above.

Michael tried to remove his hands, yet they stayed stuck to his mother's face. Helen's hair whitened, and her body became almost skeleton-like.

"What are you doing to me, Michael?" She sounded sickly, elderly, and frail.

Helen looked at Michael's face and instead found the ghostly face of her mother Elizabeth smiling eerily at her.

"That you die by your offspring," heard Elizabeth Michael said before starting to fade.

In that short plane, while transitioning between the light of life and the shadow of death, Helen understood: Michael's power reason to be to cause her demise. Elizabeth had the last laugh. She had fooled her into believing Michael could cure her only to get revenge.

Michael's hands separated from Helen's face. Helen's dead body fell to the floor.

Michael sat, sad, relieved, and enlightened. He had lost his mother. The fact she is gone would mean no more lies, abuse, and madness. The nature of his power was all too clear. If he loved, he made living things young; if Michael hated, he made them old.

* * *

Michael stood and rubbed his head for comfort. He glanced at the bed and handcuffs and was glad to be free. Helen's body laid inert on the floor. She looked old. Out of habit, Michael took the gloves and put them on his hands. He grabbed a bed sheet and covered Helen's body.

Michael started climbing down the ladder. He thought about the new information about his father. He would reach out to him.

Michael went to the laundry room and filled a small laundry bag with his clothes. He figured he also needed money.

Michael looked in his mother's purse on the kitchen counter and found the wallet inside. He took $413.00. Not much, but it would do. He picked up the kitchen phone to call his newfound dad but found no tone. Michael was not surprised. Whoever lived in that house had not been there for months. He then realized he couldn't call his dad without the phone number.

He thought it was odd there was a North Carolina phone directory on the living room coffee table. Michael searched for the "Thomas" last name in Edom until he found two "Paul Thomas" in town. He ripped the page and folded it.

He exited through the back door and walked on the sand away from the beach, searching for the main road. Michael decided against taking the Jeep because he didn't know how to drive. Helen had been adamant he obtained a license. So, he never did.

Michael walked, not knowing where to go or what to do. He then thought that making a call to his dad would be a good place to start. But first, Michael had to find a public phone. A quarter-mile down the road, he found one on the sidewalk next to the Crapshoot Motel. An older woman was using it. He only had dollar bills and needed dimes to make the call. He decided to go into the motel.

"Where am I?" Helen had driven into California in the darkness to remain incognito. He regretted being asleep because Helen wouldn't disclose their location once they got to the house.

The front desk woman looked at him as if he spoke another language. Her hair was pink, and a rose tattoo adorned her right arm.

"You are kidding me, right? She asked between strokes of gum chewing.

"No, I am not."

The clerk looked at his gloves with curiosity. "Tammy," as her name tag read, eyed him up and down. She pointed to the motel sign outside.

"Crapshoot Motel?" she asked in a condescending tone.

"That's not what I meant," Michael said, annoyed.

"You are in California," she said, crouching over the counter. She wrote on a sticky pad "California" with a heart as a period on top of the "i." She handed it to him and smiled.

"Where in California?"

Tammy shook her head and let out a big sigh, "Don't you know anything? Malibu." Michael turned to leave. He figured she was mean and wouldn't help him with anything. He would get coins somewhere else.

"I was joking. Don't be so uptight, alright? So do you want a room or not?"

Michael thought the idea of taking a shower and resting sounded good. "How much?"

"Fourteen."

"Yeah, I'll take one," he reached into his pocket and put a 20-dollar bill on the counter.

"Not that it is any of my business, but how old are you?"

"As old as you are."

"I'm sorry, but you don't look 22 to me."

"I've been told I have a babyface. Can I please have

a dollar in dimes? I need to make a phone call."

Tammy gave him the change and dimes. She went to the wall and grabbed the key labeled "22," giving it to Michael.

"Thanks," Michael said insincerely.

Michael proceeded to the room that smelled of cigarettes and wet oak. He felt filthy and went directly to the bathroom. He showered without removing the gloves. He was more afraid than ever to touch anything with his bare hands—especially any part of his body.

He dressed, going outside to the payphone. He unfolded the directory page and called the first number.

"Paul speaking, may I help you?" the male voice said on the other end.

"Doctor Paul Thomas?"

"Yes. Can I help you?"

"Dad?" said Michael.

"Who is it, Paul?" asked a female voice in the background.

"It is the hospital inquiring about a patient of mine. I'll take the call in the office."

An annoying loud beep replaced his dad's voice. Seconds later, he appeared back on, "why are you calling here?" He sounded angry. "Everyone is looking for the both of you. Where is your mother?"

"You knew you were my father, didn't you? And you never said anything?"

"Listen, it is complicated, and you wouldn't understand. My wife doesn't know about any of this and..."

"Everyone keeps telling me how everything is so complicated! I'm tired of it. I am not calling you to cause trouble, sir," Michael said with a knot in his throat filled with disappointment and a sense of abandonment. "I just need you to do me a favor. Don't know who else to call."

"What is it?" asked Paul. "Helen passed away a few hours ago, and her body still lies on the bedroom floor of a house here in Malibu. I need you to make arrangements to bury her."

"Malibu?

"Yep"

"Is the house on Beach Drive?"

"Not sure."

"Was there a red couch in the living room?"

"Yeah."

Paul shook his head in disbelief. "How did you get in there?"

"My mother broke the glass on the back door."

"Where is she? I need to speak to her this minute!"

"That won't be possible. I called to inform you she's dead. Also, to tell you, I know you are my father. But you already knew that. I need you to arrange for her body to be taken to the morgue. I can't afford it, and I can't wait for the police."

"I can't get involved," replied Paul.

"If you choose not to help me, I will call the police and tell them you had something to do with her death. Trust me, you don't want that kind of hassle in your life," said Michael. "I can make things very difficult for you."

There were a few seconds of silence followed by, "Is her body at my house?"

"I guess so. I had no idea it was your house until now. She never mentioned it."

"Okay."

"Her body is upstairs."

"Where should I tell the police to meet you?"

"Police? Meeting me? Very clever of you."

"I didn't mean it that way."

"Of course, you didn't," said Michael sarcastically.

"You will tell them I called you and told you where her body is. That I sounded upset."

"Tell me something Michael," said Paul.

Michael thought it was the first time he heard his dad calling him by his name. Too bad he was such a jerk.

"Did you kill her?"

"Why would you ask me something like that? You are the monster, not me. I would've never denied my son. But no, I didn't," replied Michael. "She died of old age."

Michael hung up, the line going dead on the other end.

"Old age?" Paul frowned. Helen was not more than fifty years old.

Paul picked up the phone and dialed 411. "Operator? Can I have the number of the Malibu Police Department?"

XVIII THE RED CARPET

The Greyhound bus stopped suddenly, its door opening announcing the 2445 or so miles ride from LA to New York City had finally ended. Michael exited, stretching his shoulders. He donned a new set of clothes and backpack he purchased on the way in a side-of-the-road store in Arizona. His brown hair and aviator sunglasses made him look uninteresting to the ordinary person walking by.

Although he promised himself, he would attempt to pass as a New York City native, the city skyscrapers made him raise his head in awe of the tall architecture.

Michael turned around when he noticed the cars traveling in the opposite direction. He raised his hand in faked confidence to hail a cab. Michael had seen it done on television; raising one's hand combined with the index finger pointed to the sky to gain notoriety against the other competing fingers pointing upwards.

One driver stopped in the traveling lane inciting the cars behind to honk in a stampede of noised frenzy.

"Drake Hotel, please."

"Okay." The cab driver lifted the lever on the meter.

Michael recalled the New York City tourism brochure he found on the bus. He left the wrinkled pamphlet behind because he didn't want to look like a tourist. The ad in the booklet advertised the hotel as one of European flavor. He had never been to Europe and figured the easiest way to accomplish it was by staying at the hotel.

Michael looked at the hordes of people crossing the street if they knew about his power. What would they do to him?

He was still troubled by the recent events; the haunting images of the youthful Claudia ripping the night with a scream, his mother's old body on the floor had been nothing less than traumatic, and his alleged father treating him like garbage.

He had no sensible explanation as to why he could do what he did with his hands. How or why, he could turn one person younger if he liked them and one older, if not so much, mystified him. He remembered the way he touched them; he placed his hands on both of their faces.

That night Michael sat at the Crapshoot Motel after speaking with his father, thinking it was time to decide what to do and where to go. He considered going back to Edom.

As much as Michael wanted to, that would've been risky, and a decision made on impulse. The desire to go back came down to finding out if Claudia's change had been permanent and, if so, trying to fix the damage he had done.

That would've been hard. To fix Claudia, he would have to dislike her to reverse the process. Even if he worked hard and developed those negative feelings, he wouldn't know when to stop touching her to revert her to 16 years old.

New York City came as a random idea. More like one with a twisted purpose. An old magazine he found in his room spoke of a charity fundraiser for Vietnamese children who suffered during the war. The event would happen in New York City in a few months involving many celebrities. Among those attending would be model Kellie Durand.

To get her to talk to him, he would go to the red-carpet event and touch her face.

* * *

Michael had been standing for hours behind the barricade. Another told him that it was the best spot to obtain an autograph or a close-up photo. Michael didn't possess a notebook nor a camera. He planned to touch her, make her younger, and get a chance to meet her in person. Michael told about three or four who came to stand next to him if they wanted to get up close and personal with the celebrities. The more people around him, the better; there would be a greater chance of coming close to her.

The vehicles started arriving with celebrities unknown to him. Soon, the line of limousines became long and slow. After another hour, he thought his favorite model would not be arriving.

A white limousine stopped, and the driver opened the rear door. Kellie appeared slowly.

Michael smiled. Kellie was everything he imagined her to be: Elegant, sensual, classy, and unattainable.

Her dark blue dress was long and beautiful.

Michael had never seen anything like it. Women in Edom didn't wear those fancy pieces of clothing.

The paparazzi kissed her with their camera flashes. She stood changing poses for what seemed forever.

Kellie then approached the crowd not too far from him and started giving autographs. She stopped signing a few feet from him, moved away from the barricade, and walked to the other side, where some guys with microphones were interviewing the attendees.

"I lost my chance," he thought.

Kellie finished the interview and walked closer to where he was standing.

"Kellie, Kellie, here!" the young woman next to him started to yell.

Kellie turned her attention to the fan. A man walking close behind her whispered in her ear and motioned her to keep moving forward.

The young woman yelled louder, and Kellie turned around. She started to approach her. Michael took his bare hands out of his pockets.

Kellie stood close to Michael. She bent down to sign a photo the teenager was holding when Michael rushed Kellie's face. The surrounding crowd gasped.

"Turritopsis dohrnii," Michael whispered in Kellie's ear.

Michael's quick act took Kellie by surprise, and she didn't immediately react.

Michael touched her for about three seconds. Kellie's hair turned from blonde to brunette. Her dress became tighter. She regressed physically a few years earlier, about the time she started modeling.

Michael didn't see the brawn bodyguard that pushed him so hard he ended up taking four more to the ground with him.

Michael got up and ran away.

❊ ❊ ❊

Michael ran to his bedroom window for the fifth time within two minutes. She was late. She was to be in front of the building at seven. It was ten after.

Michael decided he had to get a hold of himself. He thought there was no use in standing by the window and reluctantly sat down on the bed.

It had not been thirty seconds after he sat down when he heard the honking of a car horn outside. Michael jumped off, propelled by anxious emotion. He looked outside the window once more, this time finding a white limousine parked in front of the building. There were a group of kids on bicycles making sorties around the limo, wondering who was inside. Michael ran to the mirror, his feet barely touching the ground. He fixed his bow tie and hoped that Kellie would not see the suit as a rental.

The driver exited the car as soon as he saw Michael; he opened the back door for him. Michael smiled and entered nervously. The vehicle was dark with a dim light that showed a champagne bottle next to the drinking glasses. The door closed, and a brighter light came on, showing Kellie across from him. Her hair was back to blonde.

Michael's heart pounded in his chest. She looked just like the poster in his room back in Edom.

"I thought you were never going to show up," said Michael with a full grin.

The car accelerated, leaving the hotel area, but Michael did not notice. Kellie had given instructions to the limo driver before Michael entered to get to the restaurant as soon as he could.

"I'm sorry, did I make you wait?" Kellie put her hand on his leg. Her touch felt soft and warm.

"No," lied Michael, "I was just very anxious to see you."

"I was anxious to meet you too."

"Not sure what to say," Michael played with his gloves.

"You don't need to say anything. I'm taking you to one of my favorite restaurants, and there we'll have a nice talk. There are so many questions.! I will save those for later."

Michael did not reply, admiring her beauty. Kellie leaned back and looked at Michael's gloves. She was reluctant to believe Michael had been responsible for her change even though she had seen the comparison photos her team put together from before and after he touched her.

Kellie was fidgety. Something about him bothered her. Maybe it was the fact she had no logical explanation as to how such an ordinary-looking kid possessed the power of making people young again.

❊ ❊ ❊

The restaurant smelled of curry and spices. The place was commonplace for the rich and famous, making it glamorous and uptight. Word of mouth spread that it had the best Bengali food.

The restaurant manager walked away from the podium. He seemed excited to see Kellie, greeting her with a kiss on her left cheek.

"Kellie, I'm so glad you are here! I missed you so much!" the manager said in a high pitch that Michael found annoying.

"I know. I'm sorry, Dinesh," said Kellie bashfully. "It's been a while."

Dinesh put his hand on Michael's shoulder. "And who's your cute little companion? Is he your nephew?"

Michael frowned.

Kellie put her arm around Michael's shoulder; "here is my new best friend. His name is Michael.".

"Hello Killie's friend," Dinesh extended his hand with a smile. Michael shook it, and Dinesh withdrew his hand quickly, focusing his attention back at Kellie.

"The usual spot?"

"Yes, please."

Dinesh escorted them. Only a few people were dining. Dinesh stopped at a table in a corner next to a small water fountain.

"Here you go, Kellie; your favorite table," said Dinesh while pulling her chair.

"Thank you."

"And the little one can sit here."

Michael did not appreciate Denish calling him "little" a second time.

"Stop calling me that; I'm not little!" Michael sounded offended.

"Ooookay, we have a sensitive one here," joked Dinesh.

Kellie smiled. Michael stared at her, and she saw he was not amused.

"Come on, Dinesh, give him a break; it is obvious he's not little."

"Very well, friend, whatever you say," Dinesh raised his right eyebrow. "How about a bottle of your favorite wine?"

"Yes, please."

The waiter turned around and left, walking graciously among the tables. Michael adjusted his shirt, appearing uncomfortable.

"Are you okay?" asked Kellie. "You are a little on edge. Gosh, I'm sorry. I didn't mean to use that word again."

"It is fine when you say it. I know you don't mean anything by it. But yeah, I apologize for looking so out of place; I've just never been to such a fancy restaurant," Michael admired the mural on the ceiling that depicted elephants and several Indian women dancing.

"I hope you don't mind that I chose this place. It is one of my favorites."

"I don't mind. I'm glad you brought me here. Thank you. With all the cash I have in my pocket now, I would've taken you to a hot dog stand around the corner," Michael showed a childish grin.

"That sounds delightful. Yet, for our first meeting, I wanted a more intimate setting. I need to ask you in private what happened to me. I'm sure this is something you don't want others to hear."

Michael nodded. There was an awkward silence. Michael had dreamed of this moment for a long time, and now he could not find enough words to keep the conversation alive.

Kellie broke the silence first. Michael was glad she did.

"I am thrilled we found you," she was about to continue when Dinesh showed up with the red wine. He poured some for Kellie to taste.

"Thank you, Dinesh. Leave the bottle. By the way, you forgot to ask my friend about his drink."

"I'm sorry," said Denish.

"A root beer, please."

"Would you like a little one?" Denish laughed. "Relax, my friend. I'm joking. I'll be right back."

Kellie watched Denish walk away. She turned to Michael.

"Thank you for answering the ad about the "fan who touched me." If you had not said what you said at the event, we would've never found you. Hundreds called pretending to be the one. To be you."

"I learned about it in biology class. I thought it was fitting."

"I was able to remember the second word. Very uncommon. Someone on my staff looked it up and found it was about the "immortal jellyfish.""

"Yeah."

"By the way, I want to apologize for my bodyguard's behavior. He should've not pushed you that hard. They are very protective."

"It's okay."

Denish returned with the root beer.

"Thank you," said Kellie. "Would you mind giving us a couple of minutes? I'll let you know when we are ready to order."

"No problem, honey. I'll be right there," Dinesh pointed at the podium.

Kellie leaned toward Michael, placing her elbows on the table, and locking her hands.

"I must tell you; after you did what you did, I couldn't attend the charity event that night. I tried to make sense of it, and I couldn't. It was a miracle. I felt healthier. I'm hoping you tell me what you did. Once you start reaching a certain age, you pretty much kiss your career goodbye. People tell me I look younger. They keep asking the name of the plastic surgeon," Kellie giggled.

"And all refuse to believe there is no doctor involved."

"I was hoping it would make you happy."

"It did. I started to feel different after the touch. Hmm, what's the word? Flexible, I guess?" she said, looking at his hands. "So, I decided to meet you," Kellie sipped the wine, her red lipstick tattooing the glass.

She placed the glass on the table and continued, "I am like a new woman now, thanks to you. I can't stop smiling about it. I feel so much younger."

You are," replied Michael. "What I'm about to tell you may seem incredible, but it is the absolute truth."

"I'm all ears," said Kellie. Michael thought even her voice sounded pretty.

"To be honest, I have no idea how I came to have this power. All I know is that it has been sweet and sour since."

"Sorry to hear about the sour part," she interjected.

"Don't be," said Michael, grabbing the root beer. "My mother told me that when I was four years old or so, I saved our dog from dying after being hit by our car."

"How did you save your dog?"

"I touched it turned into a puppy."

"That is incredible! How did she keep your power hidden from everyone for so long? That must've been extremely difficult."

"She made me believe I had a rare disease. I grew up thinking that if I touched anything with my bare hands, I would instantly die of an extreme allergy reaction. She scared me senseless."

"Is that why you are wearing those gloves?"

"I feel naked without them. Besides, I don't quite understand this power yet. I wouldn't like any accidents," Michael's stomach growled.

"I'm sorry," said Kellie, grabbing the menu off the table. "I became so engrossed I forgot that you must be starving."

She raised her hand, and Dinesh appeared seconds later.

"Yes, Madam?"

"Today, I will have the Chingri Maach Her Malai Curry."

"Good choice as always," said Dinesh. " And for the gentleman?"

Michael looked at the menu, appearing lost in a world of foreign cuisine.

"If you like meat, may I suggest the Kosha Mang-sho? You won't be disappointed."

"Sounds good," Michael had the slightest idea what he ordered.

"Very well," said Dinesh, taking their menus and heading towards the kitchen.

"I'm going to come right out and say it, Michael; why me?" asked Kellie.

"I hope I won't scare you away with my answer."

"You won't scare me away, Michael," said Kellie, placing her hand on top of his. "I owe you the world."

"I had your posters, calendars, and magazine interviews. I would watch you on the television any chance I got. I thought I'd never been able to meet you. Once I knew I possessed this power, I figured the best way to arrange a meeting with you would be to do something extraordinary."

"Well, it worked, Michael. Here I sit across from you," she said, grabbing his hand stronger. "Can I ask you something?"

"Go ahead."

"Would you be able to make me even younger?"

"I don't know. I guess I could," Michael thought of Claudia.

"What about another person? Can you make them younger?"

"I guess."

"And what about you? Can you make yourself younger?"

Michael had not considered the idea. He doubted it.

"I am not sure. I hadn't thought about it until you asked."

"Maybe you should think about it."

"By the way, do you remember everything you have done in your life?" Michael would've preferred to ask Claudia the question.

"What exactly do you mean, Michael?"

"Do you have all the memories of years past before I touched you? I mean, how much younger do you think I made you?

"If I didn't, I wouldn't remember I had them, would I?" she smiled. "But I do remember everyone I've met recently."

"Good," Michael said, relieved.

"Well, I was looking at some old photos, and I estimate that I am about three years younger."

"That's great," said Michael, not knowing what else to say.

"Can we do this again tomorrow? Maybe at a different place? There is someone I want you to meet."

Kellie didn't want Michael to meet her husband. He was a dangerous man. She had just met Michael, yet his innocence made her feel protective. But she owed Florentino. He catapulted her modeling career, and she was successful because of it. She wondered how much longer she would have to repay her debt.

"Okay." The request made Michael uncomfortable.

Dinesh and the helper showed up with the dishes. Michael thought it looked delicious. Kellie smiled, looking intensely at him. He felt the luckiest guy alive.

XIX THE OLD MAN

The dark green car made a rumbling sound: Glaring evidence of having a hole in the exhaust. Joey liked it. His personalized license plate read "Mio," which in Italian meant "mine," but for Joey, the tag stood for "masculine, intimidating, and obnoxious."

"When are you going to fix that? It is so annoying," said Angelo pointing downward to the car's carpet with both hands.

"Fix what?" asked Joey.

"What do you mean what? The damn pipes Joey!" asked Angelo, exasperated.

"Never? It makes the car sound like a muscle car. I get a lot of looks."

"I'm sure you do."

Joey shrugged his shoulders and took a bite of a sandwich.

"And what is that you're eating?"

"A BLT, why?"

Angelo took a sandwich out of a paper bag. "A

true Italian would eat a panini."

"I'm only half Italian, remember? My mom is Greek."

"I still say you are lucky we took in a half-breed like you," Angelo said while taking a bite of his panini. "We rarely do that."

"You know I earned being here. Nothing has been given to me. You were there with me."

"I know, Joey. I'm just busting your balls."

Joey looked at the Drake Hotel entrance.

"What do you think the boss wants with this kid?"

"I don't know. He wouldn't say. Maybe he is the kid of someone who owes him big?

"Well, it has been almost three hours," said Joey impatiently.

"He told us to drive the kid to him tonight, so we gotta wait."

"Do you think his wife will be mad at him? I overheard her tell him she planned to introduce the kid tomorrow. What's his name? Michael, right? She was adamant that the boss accompanies them to dinner. She may be afraid of what the boss may do to him."

"That is not our concern. If you ask me, I think the boss thinks this kid may not be here tomorrow. I gotta make sure she doesn't see me."

As Angelo finished his sentence, the white limousine turned right at the corner. Joey bumped Angelo on the shoulder, motioning him with his chin to look forward.

Angelo opened the door. "Wait here."

Angelo jaywalked, taking advantage of the red light that stopped traffic a half-block away. He faced the wall next to the entrance and turned his head slightly. The limousine stopped ahead at the curb about 100 feet away from him.

"Thank you for dinner," said Michael exiting the limousine.

Angelo turned his head left to look at Michael.

"So tomorrow at the same time?" A voice Angelo recognized as "Mrs. Kellie" asked from inside the vehicle.

Michael nodded and shut the limo door. He walked toward the entrance of the hotel.

Angelo rushed to Michael putting his left arm around Michael's shoulders in a hold disguised as a friendly embrace.

"Hi Michael," said Angelo while giving him a smirk.

"Who are you?" asked Michael, surprised and worried.

Angelo pointed to the green car and guided Michael.

"We are in the movies. We are good friends of Mrs. Kellie," said Angelo while guiding Michael with his body to the car.

"What do you want?"

"There is someone important that wants to meet you."

"Now?"

Michael tried to get out of the grab, but Angelo pulled him tighter.

"Go in," Angelo said, opening the vehicle's rear door. Michael got in, and Angelo sat next to him.

Joey pulled out of the parking spot, the exhaust louder now.

"Who are we meeting?" asked Michael, looking up at Angelo.

"Someone very close to Mrs. Kellie," said Angelo, almost yelling, trying to overcome the loud rumble. "This Goddamn car," he mumbled.

"Why do you keep saying, Mrs. Kellie?" asked Michael curiously, hinting he was surprised.

"Why do you think, kid? Do I need to spell it for you? She's married."

Michael became anxious and angry. He didn't recall Kellie wearing a wedding ring. He was disappointed she had not kissed him. Now he understood why; she was married. Instead, as somewhat of a consolation prize, she sprayed a restaurant napkin with her perfume and gave it to him as "something to remember me by."

Michael wondered if Angelo was telling the truth. He couldn't tell. Yet, he had no reason to lie. Maybe being from a small town shielded him from being aware of people's true intentions. He hoped that wherever they were going, there would be some money proposition for him. If they were really in the movies, the prospect would be exciting.

He looked outside the car window. Snowflakes parachuted like tiny commandos dressed in white, landing on the windshield only to be pushed away by giant wiper arms.

* * *

The small airport came unexpectedly among industrial buildings. A few planes came alive by a single light above a door meant to show an entrance.

A guard opened the gate without interacting with the two in the car. The car drove in the middle of the runway to a hangar on the other side of the airport.

Joey drove the car around to the side of a huge hangar, revealing a well-lit private jet in the opening. Joey stopped the car and honked one time.

"Okay, kid. Here is where you get off. Go to the table next to the plane with a metal suitcase on top. Sit and wait."

Michael exited the car. He had a thousand questions but didn't want to ask over the loud vehicle. He figured the two wouldn't answer them anyhow.

The vehicle left after Michael shut the door. The hangar was bright and quiet. Michael sat on one of the two empty chairs at the small table.

"Why didn't she tell me she was married," Michael thought.

"Well, well, well. Here is Mr. Michael, the man, the legend, the myth right here in front of me," said a man coming out of the plane and down the stairs with a bottle of wine and a glass in one hand.

The older man wore a white suit with a floral shirt under it. His gray hair slicked back made him look like one of those people Michael had seen on the television working at Wall Street. His black shoes were shiny. He approached Michael and extended his right hand.

"I don't shake hands," said Michael.

"Of course."

"Who are you?" Michael frowned. "How do you know my name?"

"First things first. Would you like anything to drink? A glass of this fine wine, perhaps? Champagne, whiskey, beer? I have a whole bar in that plane right there."

"No, I'm not old enough to drink."

"Water, maybe soda?"

"No, thank you. Can you just tell me who you are and what I'm doing here?"

"Okay. Good. I respect a straight shooter. So, the bottom line is you came highly recommended by my wife, Kellie."

"You are her husband?" Michael thought the man could've been her grandfather. He disliked him instantly.

"My name is Florentino Accardi. Maybe you've heard of me?"

"I'm sorry. No sir."

Florentino was a mafia boss wannabe. He had attempted to join when younger but discovered he couldn't hack the life. The sight of blood made him faint every single time. The doctors told him he suffered from Vasovagal Syncope, which in other words meant he wouldn't stop passing out when exposed to blood. For that, his counterparts named him Florentino "the soft" Accardi. More as a joke than an official name. Because he was a good administrator, they allowed him to run the "aviation" branch of the organization as an associate.

Florentino had the desire to prove himself constantly. That made him sometimes reckless. A Mafia Captain had warned him to keep a low profile and not draw attention to himself.

"It doesn't matter if you haven't heard of me. I will speak in simple terms so you understand why I brought you here today. The point is that I'm wealthy. That suitcase in front of you has more money than you could ever imagine. Enough for you and your parents to buy the whole town of, where are you from, kid?"

"My parents are dead," said Michael.

"Well, then, because you don't have to split the money, you will have enough to buy a plane exactly like that one," Florentino pointed at the jet with a smile.

"It sounds too good to be true. My mom told me when something is too good to be true, it probably is."

"Not accurate in all instances. Look at what you did. Is it too good to be true? When my wife Kellie returned that night from the charity event, I couldn't believe it. I was amazed and confused. She looked like she did a few years ago. She told me the change happened after some random fan touched her. By the way, that bodyguard is now gone.

"She told me."

"Anyhow, I thought she had gone crazy. I decided to take her to a doctor," Florentino said while taking a corkscrew out of his pocket, uncorking the bottle, and pouring red wine into the glass.

"The doctor told me he couldn't explain how her body changed. A total mystery, he said. It was like she reverted to a few years back. Her appendicitis surgery scar was gone, and she had grown a new appendix! She may need another surgery to remove it, but that is beside the point. Even her wisdom teeth that were gone are there again. Somehow you got her back to 20 years old."

Michael heard his mother's voice in his head telling him what she told him one of the nights she came to visit him while he was handcuffed to the bed: "Please understand; it only takes one person to find out what you can do to put your life in extreme danger. I'm trying to protect you."

Michael looked at Florentino. "I don't know what your wife is talking about; that wasn't me, and no one has that kind of power."

"But you answered her ad. She recognized you when she saw you. Don't be afraid. You are safe here."

"What do you want from me?" asked Michael knowing there was no use in denying it.

"Well, I'm not that young anymore. I'm 67. I want you to touch me. Turn me young. Can I request to go back to 25? 21 maybe, or is that stretching it?

"I can't do it."

"You can't, or you won't? Help me understand. Is it because you like my wife? Is that it? Is that why you did it for her? You can have her and the money. What about that?"

"It's not that, well, sort of is. I like her, but I don't like you."

"What does that have to do with anything? You either have the power, or you don't."

"It won't help you if I touch you. To the contrary."

"I don't have all night, kid. I've been generous in offering you this money. I didn't have to. I could've had my guys pick you up and force you in here. I'm doing this out of respect for my wife because you changed her life. You made her younger and happy again. She was miserable. Trust me when I tell you that."

"I'm sorry, I just can't."

"I didn't want to have to do this," Florentino let out a loud whistle. Angelo and Joey appeared immediately.

"One last chance, kid. Are you going to or not?"

asked Florentino, taking off his white jacket and rolling up his sleeves.

"Please listen to me, sir. You won't like it if I use my power on you," Michael's tone changed from defiant to scared.

"Grab him," ordered Florentino looking at both Angelo and Joey.

Both grabbed Michael. Florentino put the suitcase on the floor.

"Remove the gloves. Stretch his arms on the table, palms facing each other."

Joey removed the gloves and threw them on the ground. They stretched Michael's arms on the table in front of him.

Michael groaned in pain. He felt his arms were going to come out of his shoulders. Florentino grabbed a chair and moved it close to the table. He sat and put his face between both hands.

Florentino's face made contact with Michael's hands. Michael couldn't resist looking. Almost instantly, Florentino's face became older. A white beard grew, making him look like a skinny Santa Claus.

Angelo opened his eyes wide in shock. Joey had an expression of fear.

Florentino knew something wasn't right when the joints in his hands swelled and were painful, and the pain in his lower back from kidney stones became almost unbearable. He put his right arm on his back, trying to alleviate the pain.

"Take him offa me, get him offa me!"

Angelo pulled Florentino's chair, separating his face from Michael's hands. Florentino looked about 80 years old. He had procrastinated to treat two of his front teeth that fell out of his mouth when he opened his jaw.

"Boss, are you okay?" asked Angelo.

Joey stopped holding Michael's arms unknowingly out of pure shock.

Florentino ran to the restroom without saying a word. He looked in the mirror and became enraged. He was also terrified.

He emerged from the restroom with severe kidney stones pain but walked determinedly.

"Okay, kid, I can see you don't want to do this for me. You leave me no other choice. Angelo, where are those sheers?"

"Right here in my back pocket, sir."

Angelo took out the shears and gave them to Florentino.

"Put his hands on the table."

Joey and Angelo grabbed Michael's hands.

"No. Please!" yelled Michael.

"Boss, he's just a kid," started Joey.

"Shut up if you don't want to be next," said Florentino pointing the sheers at Joey's face.

Florentino started to approach the table. He felt pain in his knees. He guessed it was from Arthritis. He looked down at the sheers and noticed his hands wrinkly and full of age marks. The thought occurred to him that if he hurt Michael's hands in any shape or form, the kid would not be able to turn him young.

"Why did you turn me into an old man?" Florentino sat across from Michael.

"I told you I can't do it for you. I don't like you."

"It only took seconds for you to ruin my life," Florentino growled but stopped himself from continuing. He wanted to threaten him with the prospect of hurting him if he didn't turn him young. To be more specific, to cut off his hands tomorrow and feed them to his dogs. Of course, if it came to it, he would tell one of his employees to do it as he wouldn't be able to stand the sight of blood. Florentino did a good job hiding the fear he felt about Michael. He reflected on his mortality, wondering how much time he had left.

"Take him back to his hotel. Let him sleep it off and bring him back in the morning."

"Boss, do you think that's a good idea?" asked Angelo. "Why not keep him here?"

"What's with you two questioning me? Didn't you hear he doesn't like me? Don't you guys see me? I'm an old man. If I make him angry more, I'll die tomorrow when he touches me. Take him back, make him happy, give him whatever he wants."

Florentino turned to Michael. "You better be ready in the morning."

Michael looked down in frustration. There was no possibility his feelings would change by then.

"I'm tired. I gotta rest. Drive him back. Stay and watch. Bring him back in the morning, " Florentino said while walking away.

"Yes, boss," Angelo and Joey said in unison.

EPILOGUE

Michael sat in his hotel room without a plan. The voices in his head sounded like his hands pleaded for him to save them from any harm.

Unreasonably, they shouted he could have touched everyone that hurt him until they died of old age. They told him in the same breath, he was not worthy of the power and deserved any bad thing that came to him, that he should have tried to escape at the hangar after touching Florentino.

He wanted to leave and get out of going back in the morning. The encounter would be bad for Kellie's husband and him as well.

Michael looked outside his window. The snow was covering the street.

The phone to his room rang. Michael thought it

was odd. He walked to it and grabbed the receiver.

"Hello?"

"Hello, Michael," greeted Kellie.

"What do you want?" Michael growled.

"I know you are angry. You have all the reason in the world to be. The truth is, I had nothing to do with what he put you through."

"But you did. You told him about my power."

"Michael, you can't be doing this to people and want it to be a secret. Everyone is going to notice. That's the reality of it. There was nothing I could've said to him that would reasonably explain my physical change. But that is not the reason I called you."

"What then?"

"You must run."

"Why?"

"He came home tonight after he met with you. You almost killed him. He says that if you don't do him right tomorrow morning, you won't be leaving there alive. I dare not repeat the things he said he would do to you."

"I'm not afraid."

"You may think so, but people like him mean it when they make those sorts of threats."

"Those two guys are downstairs."

"I know. It is snowing hard outside; otherwise, I would have my driver take me there, and I would distract them for you."

"Okay."

"What are you going to do?"

"I don't know."

"I want to say that I am very grateful for what you did to me. Please take good care of yourself. Goodbye."

The line went dead. Michael sat on the bed, stressed about what to do next. He was scared. Michael thought he in my line of work should suck it up and decide. He had tried to forget Claudia to no avail. The guilt living inside him had not gone away despite trying to escape the situation by traveling to New York City.

Traveling there was a huge mistake. It did not make anything better. On the contrary. Who was he to think he was special. He had to make it right. That would be his redemption.

He, and only he, had the power to fix the damage done to her. Nothing or no one else could make her old again. He would have to find a way to control his emotions so that they wouldn't get in the way.

With nowhere else to go, Edom was the only place he would be able to find solace. All he had to do was flee.

Michael decided the time was now or never. He grabbed his backpack and opened the room door slowly. There was not a person in the hallway.

He flew down the three flights of stairs to the front door. He leaned against the door and peeked through the glass. The car was still there, in front. Michael had hoped that wouldn't be the case.

To escape, he would have to run. Fast. Those two guys seemed committed and would indeed do anything to stop him from not showing up in the morning.

He would find a bus station to travel back home. Even if he was captured and couldn't get to Claudia, she had to find out he tried to make matters right.

Michael thought there was no time like the present. He opened the hotel's front door and started running across the street. Angelo's coffee flew out of his hand at the same time he stepped out of the car rapidly, his body halfway out of the car, "Watch out, kid!"

Angelo extended his arm out, trying to pull him out of danger as a last attempt to save him, even though he was about 200 feet away.

Michael turned his head left and saw the truck lights coming towards him. The truck driver applied the brakes forcefully upon seeing Michael's silhouette, but the truck slid forward on the icy street without slowing down.

The driver of the truck kept pushing on the brakes with no luck. The large vehicle moved with untamed force disregarding human commands. It was coming fast.

Michael covered his face with both hands, instinctively bracing for impact.

"This is the end," Michael thought with his eyes closed. "I'm so sorry, Claudia. It looks like I won't be able to make it right for you after all."

＊ ＊ ＊

Michael had heard that for some people, right before death, life flashes before their eyes. He hadn't listened to the specifics, but it must've been something like he was experiencing. While transforming into a younger self, Michael's life snapshotted like a reel going through a projector in an old theater showing a classic silent movie to an audience of one.

His mother, the gloves, Claudia, his father all flashed in scenes like completing a storyboard of his life.

Time seemed to move in slow motion. Michael felt that same tingly feeling as when he touched those who he made young and old.

Michael's body became smaller, just like when he was a small child, his clothes covering him on the ground like a tent.

"Let's go, Joey! Let's get out of here before the cops show up!" Angelo said.

"What about the kid?" asked Joey.

"He's gone," said Angelo. "Drive."

The truck went over Michael's small body without hurting him, continuing toward a metal pole. It hit it with great force, the light pole stopping it on its tracks.

*   *   *

"I hear myself crying loudly and don't know why. But great to know I'm alive.

A strange woman grabs me from the cold ground and holds me tight. She uses my shirt as a blanket to cover my naked body. I stop crying, and she starts walking like she's in a hurry. She is almost running now.

I try to speak. I want to ask the woman what's happening, but all I make are these peculiar guttural sounds I cannot discern.

The sounds a baby makes, which now I realize, I am.

I touched my face. And for too long, nonetheless. I didn't know this could be possible. I don't want to be in this body, and I don't want to start all over. I am so small."

"No worries, little guy. I'll take care of you," the woman tells me with a caring expression.

"Mom, that baby was lying in the middle of the street. Why did you take him? Whose baby is it?" asked a girl I couldn't see. She sounded young. Her breathing told me she was trying hard to keep up.

Almost a year to the date, the woman had lost her ten-year-old son to cancer. The loss had been unbearable. Pointless to say, she had not recovered—her attempts to become pregnant after losing her child had not been successful.

The relationship with her husband became contemptuous when he couldn't stop blaming her for the loss. The marriage ended with him leaving like a thief in the night.

"Good riddance," she told herself. That had been three months ago.

"Some evil person abandoned him. This little guy is going to be your new little brother. We will name him Rene. What do you think?"

"That sounds very good, mom. I like the name."

The three of us disappeared in a solitary dark alley leading to Hell's Kitchen while I touched her face, but just for a few seconds.

The End